THE WITCH'S PERIL

A Witch Between Worlds #5

EMMA GLASS

A WITCH BETWEEN WORLDS...

The vampire lords have finally come to Stonehold. Pressure builds within the occupied castle, driving wedges between all. The young lovers Elliott and Clara must reconcile their changes or push each other apart—forever. Driven by prophecies of the coming storm, Lorelei battles her curse. Nikki struggles against her insanity, and Kinsey must choose her loyalties.

Salvation and danger come intertwined. Clara is given a chance to choose her own destiny—but she must face the cunning of the vampire lords alone, stripped of protections.

It is time for the fledgling witch's fate to be decided.

ALSO BY EMMA GLASS

A Witch Between Worlds Series

The Vampire's Witch (Book 1)

Trials of the Vampire (Book 2) - Available Now

A Witch's Reunion (Book 3) - Available Now

TheWitch's Dilemma (Book 4) - Available Now

The Witch's Peril (Book 5) -Available Now

The Vampire's Gift (Book 6) Available SOON!

CHAPTER 1
ELLIOTT

The chrysm dust settled as we stared down the vampire lords. To my side Nikki Craven, and an unexpected pair in the form of Mattias Blackburn and my mother, Lorelei. Behind us all, the trio of royal guards that once guarded Clara Blackwell held the rear.

We had them outnumbered.

For now...

"Well," Nikki relaxed slightly. "*That* was a neat little trick. Teleportation without a node? You've been holding out on us."

Azuzi Akachi, lord of the Falvian Badlands—by far, my most hated opponent on the council—merely smiled with that gnarled smug grin of his. The elderly vampire stood with his back hunched and a cane under his hand; his ashy white beard dangled weakly down his chest. Of his *many* weapons, the façade of age was his favourite.

"Yes... Lord Lovrić really outdid herself this time!" As he cast her a proud glance, Azuzi spoke in that smug, casual tone that he seemed to enjoy so much. "It suggests such ingenuity…"

Svetlana Lovrić turned away in… *shame?*

After a glance among the gathered lords, he smiled darkly towards our defensive group. "I just couldn't help but notice that we appear to be *missing* one of our own. Who could that be…? I'm fairly certain we should *have* everybody here, but… why, do my eyes deceive me?"

The smug lord locked eyes with Mattias Blackburn, and a flash of something sinister crossed his expression. "*There* you are! Lord Blackburn! It would seem you've found yourself on the wrong side of this courtyard…"

Mattias steeled his gaze. "I thought perhaps I could talk some sense into our old friend."

"Is that so?" Azuzi scratched his beard. "Allow me to humor that obvious fabrication. Are you succeeding in your efforts?"

Lorelei cut in with a glare his way. "You realize that breaching this island is an act of war."

"Is it?" He asked. "I thought this was more of a *gathering.*"

Lorelei snarled. "Do not attempt to be coy with me, Akachi. There isn't a single vampire who believes you're here with *anything* less than malevolent intent."

Azuzi smiled; with those cold, calculating eyes, he never looked quite as snakelike as right then.

"Drop the pretenses," I ordered him. "Let's all save ourselves some time. Tell us why you've come."

He flashed an amused grin. "Is that any way to treat a greeting party, Elliott? Welcome back to our world! I trust you enjoyed your little *vacation?*" Azuzi lifted an eyebrow as he summed up the clothing Clara had given me—what she called my *street clothes*. "You've certainly adapted a strange sense of fashion. You certainly seem rather under-dressed for the occasion..."

All eyes were on me as I quickly calculated the odds of us surviving a direct confrontation. No matter what angle I examined, this looked bad.

*We're not getting out of here alive if we get off on the wrong foot —but **maybe** there's a way...*

"Let us speak in civility," I replied firmly. "We have cooperated as a council for millennia. Instead of spilling blood upon the soil, let us defuse the tensions..."

A few of them glanced towards me in mild interest. I wasn't quite sure what to make of that, especially as they quickly turned away.

"Defuse the tensions?" Akachi's grin dropped, along with any semblance of courtesy. "Let me remind you—you already *had* the chance to meet us halfway, Elliott. We have given you *plenty* of time to bring your precious human pet to the Council of the Eight Holds. What have you done with our patience? You stalled. You objected. You *lied* to us at every turn and banished the girl away from this world."

"You dare to question my word of honor?" I replied, baring my teeth with an angry grin.

"Do you wish to prove me wrong? If memory serves, you made us an oath to hand the girl over the *second* she returned..."

I set my jaw. I'd made that oath to buy time from their retribution. I never thought there was a chance I'd see Clara again...

"Is that true, Elliott?" Lorelei asked accusingly.

I growled in defeat. "Yes."

Disappointment filled the air around me. I felt all of my allies' eyes lock onto me in various levels of surprise and bitter frustration.

My mother snarled. "Elliott... you *idiot*."

"You're not helping," I hissed under my breath.

The lords stood in front of us; they all watched with a gamut of expressions, from utter boredom to perhaps mild amusement. Some of them clearly liked to see us squirm—a few looked sympathetic or outright annoyed.

Akachi chuckled. "*Honor* your word. Hand over the girl."

By now, I knew that Clara must be deep within Craven Keep. At my order, my vassal Kinsey had taken the human to safety, far from the bitter battle that was likely to commence.

"She isn't here," I replied without hesitation.

"Is she not?" He looked bored. "We can *all* feel when your human passes in and out of this world."

His face darkened. "Let me say this *once,* as my final courtesy—if you *dare* to lie to my face again, I will call down every vampire I have upon you. They will descend like a feast of locusts, Elliott, and they won't rest until this hold is erased from the history books. My undying, unquenchable fury will be so vast that, for centuries hereafter, scholars shall question whether Stonehold ever truly existed—from now, until the end of history..."

The other vampire lords watched him, unwilling to call him out over such a powerful threat—but equally unprepared to support it with their own. I noticed this with a small sliver of hope.

"I will tell you once more... hand her over, boy."

I sheathed my weapon and folded my arms over my chest.

"As I was saying before you so swiftly interrupted... Clara isn't *here*. She is in the castle, Lord Akachi."

He held his expression.

"If you—*all of you*—are prepared to enter this castle under a strict accord of peace, I will explain *everything* that I have discovered to the Council of the Eight Holds. You'll even get to see the human girl with your own eyes."

He simmered. "You are not in any position to—"

"That sounds amenable."

Surprised, Akachi diverted his attention to the lord of The Wastes, Valentine Vasiliev. "Lord Vasiliev? Why would you agree to such a thing?"

"Because you certainly have no monopoly over the human's fate," the *other* old and borderline villainous vampire lord spoke dispassionately. "We have no idea what this girl is capable of, short of her ability to tear a vampire lord from this world. I've seen the cataclysms we all face. The human is *profoundly* dangerous. Even so... if Elliott *did* hand her over, would we know what to *do* with her?"

Akachi narrowed his eyes furiously.

"Don't be a fool," Valentine continued mirthlessly with her characteristically withering stare. "If the young lord wishes to introduce us to the girl and speak of his discoveries, we should listen."

"That sounds logical," Svetlana added apathetically. I still hadn't nailed her angle in all of this, given that she was responsible for bringing them all here. But her tone told me that perhaps she didn't consent to this as much as her actions implied—and at this point, I was willing to ask questions later, if it meant living another day and keeping Clara out of their hands.

"I agree." Eyes-Like-Fire blankly met my gaze with an unreadable expression on her bone-pierced face. She was one of the two vampire lords I thought might be sympathetic to my position. "I am ready to hear what Lord Craven has to say."

The others merely nodded. *What is happening?*

The lord of the Falvian Badlands practically shook with rage. "You're *fools*, all of you! We are here, ready to smite this castle and take what is now so clearly and *rightfully* ours—and you wish to listen to more of Lord Craven's fairy tales?"

Mattias pushed past me. "It's the right decision—and you know it." He let his impartial gaze slide over the others. "You *all* know it. This impasse doesn't *have* to come down to a fight. None of us needs to die on this day."

Akachi openly glared. "Don't *you* start, traitor…"

"I am no traitor," Mattias replied firmly. "I act in my own self-interest, just as we *all* have for countless centuries."

"Wait."

Everyone turned to my sister.

"Don't," I whispered.

"Shouldn't I get a say in this?" Nikki licked her fangs and wickedly glanced across the gathered vampires. "I went through the Ascension. I am the rightful lord of Stonehold, and I think it would be *deliciously* fun to kill you all…"

She laughed, but I knew that she meant each and every word. For a century, her thoughts were a constant battle between peaceful sanity and wanton bloodshed. If she attacked, I knew there would be *little* of the former, and *plenty* of the latter.

Akachi replied in a disinterested tone. "Haven't you done enough killing for the day?"

All eyes fell on Nikki, taking in her blood-soaked clothing and the dark patches that had dried upon her skin. She hadn't showered after her hunt in the forests around the castle. For once, she looked just as insane as I knew her to be... and I recognized with displeasure that she was perfectly satisfied with her horrifying appearance.

"As my vassal, I order you to stand down," I said firmly.

Nikki swung round, her eyes sparkling with a mix of anger and wicked anticipation. For one brief moment, it looked as if she would attack me herself...

"You can't control me, Brother. I have tasted *true* power."

"A fledgling lord and his insane sister in a struggle for the throne," Valentine observed dispassionately. "This should be interesting."

"Enough, all of you! I am the only rightful Lord of this hold," I glared their way. "We shall not fight on this day. I have invited you all to join me inside my castle. Are we finished *posturing* in the garden?"

Akachi exposed his fangs in his smile. "...*No.*"

CHAPTER 2
NIKKI

The ancient, ebony vampire took a few steps towards us with his cane. That sick smile didn't leave his lips as his back slowly straightened with each step. My experiences with the old sage of Stonehold taught me to grudgingly respect the eldest vampires. I wondered how powerful he *really* was behind his withered and decrepit looking body.

"I shall take what is rightfully mine."

I tensed myself, licking my fangs in anticipation as I lifted my pair of faithful daggers. *These devoted blades have tasted the blood of so many enemies,* I thought with a smile. Even at my darkest, I never thought I'd see the day that they were used on a vampire lord...

Perhaps when we've finished with this old beast, we can remove Elliot from his rightful throne...

That seems like it might be counter productive... I thought to myself, taking a moment to consider the many ways I could kill this old vampire.

What amused me was how the others hung back. I'd expected them to march *with* the old bastard—but it seemed they were content to spectate from the sidelines... for now...

I couldn't blame them for their apprehension. We *all* knew what would happen: I was going to paint myself with a fresh and wonderfully unnecessary coat of spilled blood.

*I could **really** get behind that...*

A voice pulled me from my little fantasy. "Stand back."

Holding an arm out to halt us, my mother defiantly stepped forward from our group. As I glanced at her expression with mild curiosity, I saw that her eyes burned with a blazing ferocity I hadn't seen since... well... since I killed my own sister.

"What are you doing?" Elliott asked tentatively.

My attention flicked from her to the approaching vampire. *Ten more seconds at that pace, and he'll be close enough to **bite**.*

"Something I should have done a *long* time ago..."

With her defiant eyes locked onto the approaching vampire, Lorelei Craven smiled. Her curled grin made her look more like herself than anything I'd seen since I wandered back to this accursed island.

"Mum..." I started. "Let me *handle* this..."

Mother didn't answer. She marched forward in total disregard.

Lord Blackburn reached out towards her. "Lorelei, we *both* know what will happen if you—"

"Stop," she replied dismissively, pulling away and facing the coming threat. "This ends now."

Akachi Azuzi grinned that arrogant smirk he liked so much as they paused in front of one another. "Step aside. I have *business* with Lord Craven."

"I will not allow you to lay a finger upon my son," she replied distantly.

He blinked. "Are you... *challenging* us? Did that curse of yours finally destroy the last vestiges of your mind?"

"I am as in control of my decisions as I have *ever* been."

"Then... perhaps I don't understand..."

"I'm challenging *you*."

He laughed, casting a quick glance back at the other lords. None of them had moved so much as an inch, so he shook his head and turned back to his unlikely opponent.

"Akachi, you have been offered peace. If you reject my son's kind offer, I will make you *regret* that decision."

He smirked deviously. "Do you think your threats hold any meaning? You have proven yourself to be an unreliable leader, a negligent mother, and an oath-breaker. You breached the Council of the Eight Holds without fear, and you've betrayed some of our oldest and *deepest* taboos."

"What is he talking about?" Elliott demanded.

"Yes, Lorelei—what *am* I talking about?"

Mother ignored us and turned to the other lords.

"Allow me to face Lord Azuzi alone. This must happen without interference."

Valentine Vasiliev responded without the slightest hint of hesitation. "Consider this a favour repaid. But if *any* of the others move from that platform—your son, your insane daughter, or even Lord Blackburn—then I will be forced to step in. And I will show you no mercy."

Akachi glared her way. "*What?*"

Obviously disinterested, Valentine folded her arms. "A challenge has been offered. We shall not interfere."

"Cowards," Akachi glared to the rest of us.

Mother looked to Svetlana. "Do you have the ability to send us further up the island? These gardens are a memorial to my daughter. I do not wish to desecrate this place."

"I'm sorry, Lorelei. This was a one-way trip. I have to be near my machines to use them—"

"So be it," Mum sighed. "Fiona Craven was a natural fighter until her dying breath. Perhaps my eldest would prefer it this way."

"Enough rambling!" Lord Akachi snarled.

Mum took a defensive stance. "Guests first."

The elderly lord grinned evilly.

Akachi Azuzi's cane was skyward before I even realized; the illusion burst in a quick, red glow. No longer was he holding up a withered chunk of bark but a polished and menacing hook. Easily half as tall as he, it glowed with ancient etched runes along the jagged metal.

Nobody can wield such a heavy weapon effectively...

Having now abandoned any illusions of weakened limbs or physical ailment, the vampire lord brought the hook down in an incredible strike, shattering my expectations.

And it hit nothing but air.

My mother effortlessly dodged backwards in a way that I'd *never* seen a creature move, let alone a vampire. Her feet seemed to float against the ground as she shot back ten meters. Akachi was after her just as fast, swinging *hard* with his hook. Mother stopped in an instant as she dug her feet against the ground beneath her and stabilized against the mighty blow.

I thought Akachi would cleave through her bones, but my mother stopped the curved blunt edge of his hook with a single hand.

He ripped it free and repeatedly swung the massive weapon with no visible loss in stamina. Mother dodged or parried the blows with her bare limbs, taking another step backwards.

"Where is your weapon?" Akachi laughed in malice as he picked up the speed of his strikes. "You fail to take this seriously, Lorelei Craven. Are you trying to *mock* me?"

Mother glowered. "I *am* a weapon."

As the vampire lords continued their bitter dueling, I slowly lowered my daggers and relaxed my stance. In a brief glance, I turned to my stunned brother. "Should I tell her to hurry it up?"

He merely shook his head, entranced.

Everyone but Mattias had a look of astonishment. The vampire lord of Bleakwood watched the with folded arms.

I wondered what he made of this. *If I didn't know any better, I'd say he looks... despondent?*

The battle dragged on.

Akachi didn't slow his assault, but it was clear that Mum was having no trouble playing her defensive role.

"Why won't she spill his blood? Is she even *trying* to win?" I grunted.

Mattias sighed wearily. "She isn't."

That got Elliott's attention. "Why not?"

"If *either* of you hope to be respected vampire lords, you must learn to deduce these things on your own. You have eyes," Mattias replied coldly. "*Observe.*"

The stalemate continued. It seemed no attack could break through my Mum's defensive posture. She almost seemed bored with the entire thing.

"This is no fight. It is a trap."

I spun to look at Asarra, who was already sheathing her weapon as she spoke.

"A trap?" Wilhelm replied incredulously.

"Look over there," Asarra pointed across the battle.

The other vampire lords were standing idle—all of them calm and collected. A few of them were speaking among themselves, while keeping only an occasional eye on the fight.

Perhaps we should give them a reason to pay attention.

For a moment, I considered hurling one of my daggers at them. It seemed like such a *good* idea. From this range, I could drive a blade straight through one of their dark hearts.

"I'm not seeing it." Viktor shrugged in puzzlement, but he put away his sword anyway. "What about you?"

"Nope," Wilhelm followed suit. "Nothing."

Elliott's eyes opened wide with sudden realization as I forced myself to stop contemplating which of the assembled vampire lords I was going to kill first.

Wilhelm sighed. "They look bored."

"Yes, and?" Asarra replied.

"Well, they're just kind of…" His words trailed off.

Wilhelm and Viktor scrutinized the group.

Wilhelm's face fell as he watched them, completely stunned. "They're not even *paying attention!*"

"If this was a *truly* a duel for the fate of Stonehold," Elliott observed dryly, "they would treat it as more than a curiosity. They *let* Akachi do all the talking. This isn't a battle, it's a *setup*."

"Maybe there's hope for you yet, Lord Craven," Mattias replied, concentrating on the duel.

I pointed. "It's happening."

"What's happening?" Wilhelm asked.

Elliott descended into a grin.

Our mother sidestepped a fierce blow of Akachi's swinging hook, thrusting a curled, glowing hand into Lord Akachi's face. The vampire lord recoiled with rage, dropping his hook to the ground.

"My eyes!"

Elliot tilted his head. "Did she just *blind* him?"

"Yes," I observed. "And now she can move in for the *kill...*"

Lorelei wasted no time. As her enemy staggered angrily, she moved around him in dancelike motions, drawing prepared spell-tags from within her loose clothes. Each one of them hovered in the air as she spun with grace and precision. The ruler of the Falvian Badlands seemed to be recovering his eyesight, tracking her movements and raising his hands for an attack that never came. Mother took a small leap back and thrust out her palms.

"Lorelei—what is—?"

Comprehension dawned on him just in time.

"Stop!"

Mum thrust her hands together.

The spell-tags lit in a small, blue blaze, then slammed onto Lord Akachi's body. While they didn't burn him, they dropped him to his knees and forced his hands behind his back.

He fought for control, but it was to no avail.

"It's a binding charm..." I realized aloud.

Powerful enough to restrain a vampire lord? How is that even possible?

I didn't have an answer for that.

It didn't matter. The battle was over.

The lord of the Falvian Badlands furiously worked to

wrench himself free. Humiliated and forced onto his knees, he let loose a bitter growl.

He was at Lorelei's mercy, and he knew it. In an instant, he was surrounded by the remaining lords, but they were showing no sign of displeasure.

"What are you doing?" Akachi Azuzi snarled. "What are you waiting for? Attack her and release me! Let us assault this castle and take what is rightfully—"

"Be quiet," Valentine ordered, backhanding him.

Akachi glared up at her in stunned silence.

"You had your chance," Eyes-Like-Fire glared down at him. "We warned you to take the path of *peace*, Lord Azuzi—but you would not listen to reason..."

"You were always the one to foster conflict, Lord Azuzi. That cannot be abided in these delicate times," Lorelei added.

Akachi began to comprehend the full magnitude of what had happened.

"We have enjoyed a fragile balance," Ooktum Krum spoke. From what little I knew of the old, silent shaman, his input came at such rare occasion that it nearly warranted breaking out the *good* bottle of wine. "You have chosen to disrupt that balance for your own selfish gains—and that decision bears *consequences*..."

"All of you, *traitors!*" Akachi incredulously swore.

Chanda Song glanced down at the conquered lord. "Says the vampire lord who would plunge this world into darkness over a *girl*."

The rest of us stared.

Elliott, in particular, looked astonished.

I came here to warn him of their threat—a threat that he saw coming but wasn't prepared for.

*What if they were **never** a threat to us?*

*What if I was **wrong?***

The very possibility boggled the mind. I could tell his entire worldview was being completely shattered and rebuilt right before his very eyes...

Does this mean we're not going to kill them?

I laughed aloud at my own internal conflict, pushing the voice down deep where I could ignore it for awhile. My royal guard friends eyed me with equal parts suspicion and curiosity, but they didn't say anything as the vampire lords approached.

Svetlana Lovrić stopped at my mother's side, her face lit up with a smirk.

"Now that we have *that* loose end taken care of... how about we *finally* get down to business?"

CHAPTER 3
ELLIOTT

For me, it was privately a moment of personal justice that everything came full circle for Akachi Azuzi. He was bound into the very same dungeon cell that previously held my old friend Sabine—the traitorous sorceress who secretly and indirectly served him—and cast into sleep until I could decide his fate.

Considering that *his* arrival in my castle set off the small chain of events that led directly to Clara's coma, I considered it fitting that Akachi should suffer the same fate.

"Will that be enough?" I asked, gazing over him. Of course, it didn't *look* like he was going to be waking up anytime soon —but our previous tenant had figured out a way to escape justice in the form of magical suicide

It was a mistake I would not repeat.

"Counting Nikki Craven and yourself, *nine* vampire lords donated power to seal Lord Azuzi into slumber," Eyes-Like-Fire observed with an amused smile. "Yeah… I'm pretty sure that's gonna be enough."

"You raise a valid point."

"I'd rather raise a glass of blood. I am *starving*."

Chanda Song laughed nearby. "Tell me there's going to be a feast? I've never been to Stonehold, and I'm looking forward to trying your food."

Lorelei averted her iron gaze from our sealed and sleeping prisoner. "The kitchen is hard at work preparing an appropriate meal."

"Oh good!" Chanda grinned widely. "I cannot wait!"

"Now," Lorelei continued, "if you'll all excuse me, I must take leave for a while. My children can lead you to the grand hall. The first course should be ready shortly."

"Really?" Svetlana asked. "But what about—?"

"My progeny will fill you in. *He* can help."

"He?" Nikki asked.

Lorelei nodded to Lord Blackburn.

Half the lords—Nikki and myself included—turned to Mattias with a curious scrutiny. He cleared his throat. To the unspoken questions, he replied: "Let us break bread before we discuss matters further."

Nikki and I glanced shared a questioning glance.

As she moved to leave, Lord Blackburn followed her away from the group and took her arm. It seemed none of the others found this curious—but I did. I intended to listen in on their conversation, but the other lords commanded my attention.

"We haven't forgotten your insolence," Valentine Vasiliev glowered at me for a moment. "Lord Azuzi may have been misguided, but his accusations stand true. You have plenty of explaining to do, little lord. We've entered your castle on terms of peace, but I certainly expect answers."

Great, I thought dejectedly to myself. *Glad to hear that the vampire lords may still be troublesome after all.*

"I understand," I replied. "All will be explained."

"See that it is," she scowled menacingly.

My attention diverted back to Lorelei and Mattias—but she was already gone. With no small help from miserable old Lord Vasiliev, that window of opportunity flickered into nothingness.

I made a mental note to ask Lorelei about it later.

For now, all of my enemies in the world were here in my castle—and we were about to have one of the most interesting dinners I'd ever experienced...

⚜

THE GRAND HALL WAS FILLED WITH THE SOUNDS OF MERRIMENT as my surprise guests drank the finest blood on offer in the chilled castle cellars.

As the feast began to hit the table, I excused myself long enough to summon over Wilhelm Nettleshire from his guarding place near the door. It hadn't escaped my notice that Clara's guardians were released back into the castle from their posts abroad, and I hadn't yet decided what to do with them. They had proven themselves borderline useless against any *real* threat in the castle...

"Wilhelm," I acknowledged him.

"Ah! Lord Elliott! I don't recall if I had a chance to properly welcome you back to Stonehold," he cheerily bowed his head to me. "How might I serve, my Lord?"

I sighed. "This threat seems to have subsided for the moment..." I gazed over my shoulder at the gathered vampire lords, still trying to make heads or tails out of this. "Bring me Clara Blackwell. They will want to meet her shortly, and I can't stall for long."

"As you wish," he replied dutifully. "Shall I, err, take the other two with me? She'll undoubtedly want to see Viktor and Asarra again—"

"No," I ordered. "Just you. Now go."

Wilhelm nodded, disappointed. "Of course."

Once he was on his way, I cast a dark glance toward the other two. They pretended to not hear as they stared straight ahead, fading back into the passive trance that was so characteristic of the royal guards.

I returned to the head of the table. Nikki, curiously, had decided to forgo the seat. Instead she sat at my side, across from the empty space that would soon belong to Clara and Kinsey.

What a mess, I thought to myself. *I'll have to figure out where I stand with my sister, since she's been made a proper vampire lord...*

I wondered what the others assembled here thought of my predicament. It was clear that there would need to be a reconciliation of some kind, but in the time since Nikki's little momentary disrespect in the courtyard, she'd remained silent —and I wasn't in any hurry to start picking apart a succession crisis over dinner.

At least she'd *finally* showered off and changed her blood soaked clothing...

I closed my eyes, ignoring all of my problems for just one brief moment. Somewhere on the edge of my awareness, I could feel Clara's presence... and it soothed my worries.

I don't care what it takes. We will get our happy ending...

Had I known the trouble that lay in wait, perhaps I wouldn't have been so swift to make such promises...

CHAPTER 4
CLARA

I paced back and forth across Elliott's suite in despair. At the door, the young female vampire quietly stood guard. At least she was taking this seriously—instead of doing that *zoning out* thing the royal guards could do, Kinsey was on red alert.

I wish I had more time, I thought despondently. *If I could have learned some proper magic, instead of relying on this old book... I could've* **stayed.** *I could've* **fought.**

With the vampire lords here in the castle, it seemed like any chance to explore my own abilities was vanishing right before my very eyes...

"We have to *do* something," I moaned. *"Anything!"*

"We *are* doing something," the girl grumbled. "We are keeping you far away from the battle." She cast me a surprisingly filthy look. "Unless you've forgotten, human, you are the *entire* reason that they are here."

"I haven't forgotten," I replied numbly.

"Maybe it would be better if you *had*," she grunted.

I sighed. *Every time we come together, it all falls apart around us. Is this another cycle I'm doomed to repeat?*

"You could have spared us all a lot of grief."

I wilted. "Wait. What is *that* supposed to mean?"

Kinsey scowled, shaking her head.

"Do you have a problem with me?"

The guard smirked, pushing off from the wall. "Of course I have a problem with you. Why wouldn't I?" Her smirk turned to bitter irritation as she stared me down. "In your absence, I've watched my liege turn into something he isn't..."

"And what would that be?" I defiantly asked. *If I'd given that just a **little** more thought, I could have realized I might fear the answer...*

"A tyrant," she replied darkly.

"My Elliott? That's impossible."

"*Your* Elliott?" The guard snorted.

"Yes," I confidently smiled. "Mine."

"Let me remind you, little human—while you may have spent a few days with Lord Craven, *we* have been dealing with his behaviour the past twelve months. And it *wasn't* easy."

My smile faltered. "What do you mean?"

Kinsey averted her eyes in thought for a moment, and I suddenly felt a strong sense of dread. *Whatever it is she's talking about—she **believes it**...*

"Whatever effect you *think* that you have on him, it brought out the *worst* in Lord Elliott in your wake. He turned into a shadow of his former self—bitter, merciless, and devoid of rational thought. His decrees darkened, and he ruled this hold with an iron first…"

She took a furious step closer to me, overwhelmed in anger. I was nearly taken aback by her fury. "I *fought* beside him in the Dawning Mines. I saved his life, and he saved mine. While *you* slept in this castle, we faced a beast that could have ended us both…"

"The… tatzelwurm?" I asked. "You were *there?*"

"Elliott Craven should have died in that miserable cavern," the guard despondently shook her head. "*All* of us should have died down there… instead, we endure. I've regretted it—all of it."

"All of *what?*" I asked carefully.

Her eyes flashed at me. "If I'd known what my Lord would become—to what depths I'd watch him fall, I would have let the hellish darkness of the Dawning Mines become our tomb."

Her admission swept the breath from my lungs.

"You'd let Elliott… *die?*"

"I can see it in your eyes. Don't you *dare* judge me," Kinsey growled in her conviction. "You weren't here! Think of me whatever you want, little human—but you have no idea what havoc your presence on this world has wreaked. On my Lord's orders, I will stand here and protect you with my final, dying breath… but that doesn't mean I have to *forgive* you… you have cost this hold so much."

"I didn't want to go," I replied firmly.

"It doesn't matter. Lord Craven fell *victim* to your unnatural appeal. No one should ever wield this kind of power over a vampire lord. You have cast Stonehold into chaos."

She smirked mockingly, shaking her head. Mighty vampire or not, I was ready to just slap the ever-living hell out of her for this attitude. "You don't even know the *first thing* about this world, do you? Such a foolish, deluded creature— no *wonder* you so casually ignore your own accountability…"

A banging at the door stopped us in our tracks.

Kinsey snarled. "Password?"

I'd recognize that voice anywhere. "Seven slithering snakes slide southbound, singing sixteen silly songs—"

"Stop it," she growled. "Don't do that."

The voice laughed.

"If you're not going to take this seriously…"

"Fine. The password is *Password!* With, what was it, the number for *1* at the end? And the whole word is lowercase? He says that's important."

I almost burst out laughing.

Begrudgingly, the guard unlocked the door. With a huge grin on his face, Wilhelm wandered into the room. "I suppose *you're* responsible for that one?"

I laughed. "It's, uh, a joke on my world."

"A joke? It's a pretty lame joke."

"It's a pretty lame password."

"Really? Because I'd have *never* guessed it."

I shook my head in amusement. "I'll explain it later. Tell me what's going on out there. We haven't heard anything since we saw that crazy cloud in the sky…"

"Why spoil the surprise?" He shrugged aloofly. "Both of you have been summoned to the grand hall. Dinner is served."

"Oh really?" The guard glared, clearly unconvinced. "Second dinner tonight? I guess our kind and loving Lord might be feeling *hungry*…"

I could feel the venom in her voice.

"Yeah, well, the castle is just *full* of guests tonight. Admittedly, the kitchen staff's a little tired, but when somebody told them all the vampire lords were joining us for a classic Stonehold feast, they cleaned up their tune *real* quick." He sighed when he realized what he'd said. "Well, there goes the *surprise!*"

"The... vampire lords are inside the castle?

The guard sighed. "I guess *that* defused quickly."

"Seems like it! We've got one in the dungeon. He's out like a light in a magical coma and buried in enough binding charms to make a regular vampire sick for *weeks*." He turned to me with an amused look. "Look at you, little trendsetter! Seems like *magical comas* are a real hit! But, if you'll take a little constructive criticism, how about aim a little lower next time? Personally, I would have settled for a new hat or something..."

⚜

WILHELM ESCORTED ME DOWN THE STAIRS OF CRAVEN KEEP AS Kinsey reluctantly followed behind. No matter how his infectiously jovial personality cleared the air, I couldn't help but wonder about the things she'd said.

"Wilhelm... how was Elliott when I was gone?"

"Are you sure you want to know?"

The pit in my stomach deepened. "I think so."

He kept up the smile. "Well... I wasn't really around for that, so I've only got the odd story or two to go off of. It sounded pretty rough."

"You weren't around? Where were you?"

"The mainland," he replied quietly.

"You weren't in the castle?"

"No, none of us were. Not Viktor, Asarra, or me."

"Why not?" I asked, fearing his response.

"Lord Elliott can hold a grudge. When his *doting* little sister overpowered the three of us and left us battered in the stairwell, then took you down to the dungeons? Lets just say he blamed *us* for that.

I stopped in my tracks. *"What?"*

"Oh, he was in a bad mood," Wilhelm replied with a small chuckle—but the smile slipped from his face. "Our esteemed ruler decided that we had to be *punished...*"

"But *Nikki* did that! If anything, it was *her* fault!"

"Yes, well, she was punished too. Remember the bit where he had her birthright taken away from her? She didn't really get off scot-free. Not that it mattered in the end, by the looks of things. The fools in the castle made her a vampire lord in his wake, so... I'd say she came out ahead..."

I struggled to believe this. It seemed unlike the man I'd grown to love, but I knew Wilhelm would never lie to me.

Kinsey clearly enjoyed my clear discomfort. "Don't act too surprised. The moment that you left this world, Lord Elliott went to a dark place—and it only worsened as the months dragged. Whatever kindnesses you think that you cultivated within our master, they withered in his cold heart... and we *all* paid the price for it."

"Wilhelm?" I turned to him despondently.

He hesitated. "The loss affected him in ways none of us could have foreseen. From what I hear, even the Sage of Stonehold went into a funk—he hasn't left the castle library in *who knows* how long." That's when Wilhelm paused for a moment, collecting his thoughts. I grew nervous at what he was about to say. "That night *changed* Lord Elliott."

"It *changed* him?" I squeaked, holding back tears.

"Yes. I'd even go so far to say it *broke* him..."

I didn't know how I was supposed to react to all of this. I

knew he'd been hurt. We *both* had. But Elliot had told me precious little about what had happened in my absence...

"We'd better get a move on," Wilhelm noted, trying to cover himself with an awkward grin.

Disappointed and dismayed, I fell into step beside the former guard as we continued down the staircase that had apparently doomed all of my friends.

"Where did you all go?" I asked despondently.

"Nowhere we couldn't handle..."

"What about Victor?" Kinsey glowered.

"Fine, Victor was sent to a settlement that had run into some trouble."

Kinsey snarled. "Lord Elliott forced Victor to stand guard above the Dawning Mines."

"What?" I gasped.

"Maybe it was a *little* cruel..." Wilhelm blanched.

"One guard, left as a single line of defense in case another tatzelwurm popped up. It's one of my very darkest nightmares —a monster that fell to nothing short of himself, a vampire lord. Our great and loving lord decided to put a *single* guard there."

"Everything worked out..." Wilhelm added, trying to keep things somewhat positive.

I felt sick to my stomach. I couldn't fathom Elliott doing something like this, but I knew they were telling the truth. It made me question the time that we'd spent together in my house... all of that time caring for his burns, showing him my world...

*Is **that** what I do to him?*

*Do I make him better, only to make him... **worse?***

The rest of the long walk was done in silence. Wilhelm and

Kinsey escorted me across the castle bailey, careful to avoid the main village on our way into the main stronghold.

From there, it wasn't far to the grand hall. When Kinsey knocked on the door, I was surprised to see Elliott personally greet us.

"Welcome back, Clara," he smiled reassuringly.

I swallowed back my fear and I merely nodded with a faked smile. "Glad to *be* back…"

"Well," Kinsey crossed her arms sternly. "So long as you don't require me further tonight, I'll just—"

"Nonsense," Elliott replied. "You are my vassal. Stay here and eat with us. There's a chair waiting for you."

"I've already eaten," she observed dryly.

They shared a look. I noticed Elliott narrow his eyes and set his jaw. "Kinsey, you're aware that I don't take kindly to being tested…"

I felt my spirits crumble. *He really **is** a shadow of his former self.* I could barely keep myself from bursting into tears. *When you sent me away from your world... what did you become?*

"Fine," she finally replied. "Second dinner it is."

The vampire blinked his attention back to me with a warm smile that only twisted the knife harder. Lightly pushing the doors further apart, he turned to me with a kinder air. "Clara, I want you to meet some friends."

Elliott placed his cold, hard hands on my shoulders. Drawing me into the room, he stepped aside. My eyes widened as I finally saw them all for the first time. The seated group of vampires rose from the table—each of them more spectacular than the last.

"Fellow vampire lords… this, is Clara Blackwell."

CHAPTER 5
ELLIOT

The extrasensory awareness of Clara's presence was almost overpowering, and I knew that I wasn't the only one experiencing this feeling. All of the assembled vampire lords seemed to be lost in thought as I led her to a seat at my side.

"So, *this* is the human we've heard so much about," Svetlana peered curiously from a few seats away. "You look more like us than I expected…"

Clara was briefly bashful. "We aren't all that different, I guess."

Elbows on the table, Svetlana clasped together her hands, resting her chin atop them with a dreamy smile. "What I'd give to *properly* study you. I'm sure that human biology is *fascinating*…"

"There's no need to scare her," I replied dryly.

"What is this feeling?" Lord Vasiliev asked. "It's as if I can sense *everything* in this room…"

"Yes," Eyes-Like-Fire turned towards us with a look I couldn't quite read. "I noticed that as well."

Clara disappeared into her first few bites of charred poultry as I tented my fingers, turning toward the lords. "I've taken to calling the feeling *extrasensory perception*, for lack of a better phrase." I casually explained. "I don't know what causes it, or why. Whenever Clara is near me, I feel bombarded with these sensations. It was… rather distracting at first, but you grow accustomed to it…"

Chanda bit into her slice of crisp vegetable pie with an expressive look. "You don't say…"

"I barely think about it anymore. It gets much easier to ignore with time."

"And this effects all vampires?" Valentine asked.

"None of my servants have noticed the effect… and my sister never gave me the impression that she sensed this before. It's a sensation that might be unique to vampire lords…"

They all turned to Nikki. She'd just taken a swig of blood, and quickly swallowed it. "Yeah. What he said."

"Fascinating," Svetlana observed.

"We are straying from the matter at hand," Ooktum Krum noted sternly. "Lord Elliott, now that you bring us the human, it is time to discuss the future…"

Clara froze, halfway in a bite.

They all stared our way in unified agreement.

"We can speak of the future, but first, I need to understand the past. I'm not afraid to admit that I expected a battle in my courtyard upon your arrival. What is the true reason behind your cordial behavior?"

A few of them shared looks.

"It was your mother," Eyes-Like-Fire replied.

"Lorelei Craven?" I raised an eyebrow. "Explain."

"She came to us, one by one," Svetlana explained. "Surely, you are aware that she has been on a pilgrimage..."

"She left Stonehold without saying a word. I had no knowledge of her whereabouts."

"Really?" Chanda tilted her head.

"Yes," I replied firmly.

"That's not like her," Svetlana rebutted.

"Tell me," I responded, swishing my glass of blood. "How was my mother acting, before she abdicated the throne? Was she out of the ordinary? Most of you would know, given her long reign..."

Valentine sat back, folding her arms. "Your mother is something of a... *complicated* woman. It was not quite unexpected for her to grow weary of the world, but I'll admit that the suddenness was rather strange."

"Right," I nodded in agreement. "You see, while the *rest* of you remember her from her time on the council, and my sister here came back into the picture just a year ago... *I* have been dealing with her changes on a daily basis. Lorelei has been steadily growing further detached."

"Is that so?" Eyes-Like-Fire scratched at a piercing. "That explains a few of your choices..."

"She has been traveling," Valentine explained dryly. "As far as I'm aware, the only hold she didn't venture to visit was the Falvian Badlands. Lord Azuzi did not make her feel particularly welcome there."

"And what was the purpose?"

"Uniting this world," Ooktum answered.

"For what purpose?"

Chanda sipped her blood. "To rally with you."

I hesitated. "Why would she...?"

Valentine scowled. "The world is on the cusp of destruction. Lorelei has convinced us that you... and the human girl... may hold the key to our salvation."

She matched eyes with my beloved.

Had I so badly misjudged them?

"To be clear, this is a recent decision," Ooktum quietly replied. "Your mother worked tirelessly to change our minds. She told us about the things she saw in the Pierced Veil..."

"You knew?" Mattias cut in.

Valentine chuckled. "*Of course* we knew."

"But... at the council—"

Ooktum shrugged. "We played our parts. Lord Azuzi is easier to... guide... when he believes that he is in full control."

"So... you united against him?" I asked.

Svetlana nodded. "He reveled in the destruction wreaking our world. Azuzi saw opportunity in our peril, and a chance to expand his own hold. He would have gladly cast us all to the wind if it meant getting his hands on the girl. The rest of us didn't particularly care for that level of... *indiscretion*."

"I never would have believed it possible—that my mother could could sway you all, or that she would bother to try."

"We owe her a debt of gratitude," Mattias replied. "Your mother will be remembered for her role as a peacekeeper. Even before you were born, she worked to protect us all from dangers you cannot begin to fathom. None of the respect she was given came from a place of pity. It was hard earned."

"That's right," Chanda agreed. "She has traveled down a strange path, but Lady Craven is a deeply fascinating woman. I don't think she cared much for spending time in Alevorra, though. Our hold has been peaceful for many years. We might lack a sense of urgency..."

"Lord Song, you wouldn't know danger if it swam up and bit your rear," Ooktum observed wryly.

Everybody laughed—even *she* did.

When the laughter subsided, Eyes-Like-Fire looked my way. "Lord Azuzi stirs conflict for power. Power, for power's sake, is *always* his goal—and he couldn't be allowed to thrive in his position. Lorelei Craven shared powerful knowledge with us—and she asked that we support her, when the time came. By supporting *her*, Lord Elliott... we supported *you*."

"I cannot thank you all enough for your willingness to join with us here in Stonehold. All this time, I've feared the worst... but now, I see that I was mistaken. I can promise you that I will hold no secrets from my fellow lords," I replied.

"No more secrets," they all noted in unison.

Clara remained as quiet as before. She ate her food, lost in thought as she merely watched the rest of us. To be honest, most of them were watching her right back—so it was a *mutual* sort of scrutiny.

It was Svetlana Lovrić who broke the silence.

"Clara Blackwell... do you wish this world *harm?*"

"What?" She nearly choked on her forkful of food. "Of course not! Your world is *fascinating*, and *incredible*, and it's... all the things my world isn't."

"Go on," Svetlana motioned, rolling her hand.

Clara began to stare into space as she compiled her thoughts, and a dreamy smile crossed her lips. "There is a sense of magic I can't begin to describe. I can feel it in every blade of grass and every breath of air. Even the sky in this world is incredible. It's my favourite thing to see when I'm here. I've missed those stars so much—those stars, and those swirling colours, and how the sunshine fades away the higher up you look… the beauty of your cosmos is always here, even during the day. It makes the sky in my world look dark and dangerous. It pains me to leave this place… as if a piece of me is firmly rooted in the soil, no matter how far I travel."

"Did you *pain* you to leave Lord Elliot behind in this world?"

Clara froze.

"Don't act as if you don't understand, young Clara," Lord Blackburn sternly chided. "As the Council of the Eight Holds, are keenly aware that you maintain a quite a *curious* attraction to one another. It was one of the reasons we were willing to overlook Lord Elliot's…" He paused for a word. "*Frustrating* choices."

"However, our understanding comes at a fair cost," Ooktum Krum continued firmly. "One we expect you to pay, if this new alliance is to be forged."

I swallowed hard, a small ball of anger rising within me.

Svetlana glanced between us and laughed. "You are quick to draw conclusions. This was always your flaw, Lord Craven. We have no interest in separating you from your precious human. We are looking for something far more valuable…" She leaned over the table, folding together her long fingers. "Answers."

"Answers?" Clara asked quietly.

I already knew what she meant. "Of course."

"For now, you will tell us what we want to know."

"Which is?" Nikki asked curiously.

Svetlana's eyes flashed between us. "*Everything.*"

Clara and I shared a look. We agreed to adjourn for twenty

minutes, aware that this would be a *long* night. I clicked my fingers for a server, requesting a fresh mix of awakening herbs to light for the table. When the vampire lords had returned, the roasted scent of the herbs had filled the hall. Despite my exhaustion from this longest of days, I'd bought myself a few hours of attentiveness.

I got comfortable, and Clara began to speak:

"It started with an abandoned lake…"

CHAPTER 6
CLARA

Whenever Elliott described the vampire lords, he always painted a picture of *dread* around them.

I found that he was deeply mistaken.

There was nothing horrible or fearsome about them. Clearly, they were powerful... but whatever he saw in them to inspire such wanton fear, it was lost on me.

If anything, they seemed quite eager to meet me; and in their fascination, they were willing to listen and to *learn*. The lords and I held a mutual interest that only deepened as I spent hours telling them of my world...

They had so *many* questions.

When the night was strong and the herbs had fully burned out, we rose from the long-forgotten feast. All seven of the vampire lords greeted me one by one, taking my hand in theirs and expressing various forms of gratitude for the chance to talk... but it was clear there was still much to discuss in the morning.

"Right!" Nikki declared as she widely stretched out her

arms with a long yawn. "If you're all *satisfied* for the moment, I'm happy to help you to the Chrysm portals."

"Do you think we'd so quickly leave this place?" The elderly female lord asked, casting her a deceptively serene smile. In a glance, I thought that I saw something menacing shift beneath the surface, and it made me instantly reassess my first impression.

They all seem so benevolent and curious—but clearly she hides ferocity behind those eyes.

"Yes," Nikki tilted her head. "Were you not...?"

Elliott hastily took over, eager to save face. "There's no reason to be *rude,* Nikki. You are all welcome to stay on the Isle of Obsidian as our official royal guests, until such time as you are ready to return to your holds..."

Nikki shot him a filthy glare—thankfully, it went largely unnoticed by anyone else in the grand hall.

The elderly lord callously narrowed her standoffish eyes. "Do not perceive our cooperation as docility, young Lord Elliott. There is still a great deal for us to discuss. Fanciful descriptions of the many wonders of the human world are fascinating, but they bring us no closer to solving the calamities that have engulfed our holds, and *none* of us have forgotten that a vampire lord rests in your dungeon. We cannot leave this castle while *that* little thread remains unresolved..."

The vampire lords nodded in solemn agreement.

Even after our time apart, I understood Elliott Craven enough to see the way his mind processed things. So much happened in the blink of a passing second. While his expression barely faltered, I felt a great deal of turmoil bubble beneath the surface. It was clear that he felt this was a pivotal moment—even if the impact was lost on his annoyed sister.

"Forgive us," Elliott bowed gracefully. "It has been a long day, and I am exhausted from my journey between worlds."

The elderly vampire—Lord Vasiliev—lifted her chin and stared down at him. Seeing him humble himself before them made me irrationally angry—but he had enough on his plate just keeping Nikki on her best behaviour.

The last thing that he needed was for *me* to add fuel to the fire, no matter how tempted I was... and despite the energizing night, I still couldn't get out of my head what Kinsey and Wilhelm had been telling me.

"Of course," the elderly vampire lord replied coolly. "We can continue this at sunrise."

"Thank you for your understanding," Elliott agreed. "I'll be happy to escort you to our finest guest quarters. I must warn you, however—it is rare that we have guests of your stature, and I cannot guarantee that the accommodations available will befit a vampire lord..."

"I'm sure we will make do," beautiful Lord Song smiled softly. "We'll leave you to your rest."

Lord Vasiliev held a halting hand up. "Not quite yet."

Elliott lost the strength to keep his expression from visibly dropping. "Is there something else?"

"The portal," she replied firmly.

"The... portal?"

"You've disabled it. Before I retire for the night, I want to see evidence that you have rectified that situation..."

The look on Elliott's face said—*You're joking.*

Nikki sighed, tilting her head in annoyance. "Do we *really* have to do that this now?"

"Let them sleep," Svetlana offered. "It can wait until the morning, can't it? We have *already* kept the Cravens occupied for the better part of the night…"

The matronly vampire was clearly unmoved. "I think some assurance of quick passage back to our holds isn't out of the question."

Elliott was clearly weighing the decision, but he finally spoke. "If you'll all accompany me, we can see about getting that chrysm portal back online…

"Can I come?" I asked hopefully.

"You want to see the portal?" Elliott teased.

I was slightly offended by his tone. I knew he didn't mean to condescend, but the revelations of his choices during my time away had me questioning my feelings. I recognized that this was *probably* not the best time to call him out on that… but I certainly wanted to see how he handled himself in front of the other vampire lords.

Elliott's face subtly hardened.

"Of course you can come!" Nikki broke in, clearly frustrated by Elliot's strange hesitation. I suddenly felt as if I'd missed something unspoken, but I followed along all the same.

𝕺𝕷𝕭

NIKKI LED THE WAY TO THE NEAREST CHRYSM TELEPORTER node. With the size of the group, the two Cravens had to split the transport party in half to bring us all safely to the main chrysm hub beneath the castle. I went with Elliott's group, which included the tribal nomad Eyes-Like-Fire, the beautiful and angelic Chanda Song, and the mysterious shaman Ooktum Krum.

The teleporter hub always struck me as something foreign to this world, as if a complex machine from the future had been placed at the heart of an ancient castle. The nodes were collected in groups of five, each one large enough for several people to stand upon as they faced down a brief hallway of industrial darkness. The halls convened on the center of the hub, an impressive tower of gigantic magical walls that displayed charts and information I couldn't decipher. Above and spreading from the tower were hundreds of clear pipes filled with glowing red liquid—chrysm ore, I guessed—that out from the chamber, webbing across the ceiling and lighting the whole atrium in a strange and terrifying glow.

The two vampires at the controls barely paid any of us mind—which was interesting to me, as so many of this world's leaders were now standing before them. Something told me if the leaders of my own Earth wandered into the ground control station at NASA, the people there would be deeply interested in the reason for their visit... but here, not a single soul seemed to care.

Then again, these vampires *did* seem rather dedicated to their task. Perhaps there was magic at work.

Within the shadows of one particularly dark wall, we passed through a hidden door. It took us to an ominous staircase, with mysterious fog flowing over our feet as we ascended to a thick glass platform. Beneath us lay a barely moving vacuum of dark red chrysm. Some kind of gigantic jagged flat pincer stuck straight up and out from the platform in front of us. Nearby, a vampire in a strange helmet was flexing her fingers in a pair of gauntlets that matched her metallic faceplate.

"What are *those?*" I asked Nikki.

"The armor?"

"Yeah."

"The gatekeepers need special equipment to manipulate the chrysm in this chamber," she explained. "I have *absolutely* no idea how it works. You'd have to ask our mum about that... or Lord Lovrić."

"I think I will..."

The gatekeeper turned to our party and hesitated.

"My... my *lords!*" She bowed.

The vampire lords gave her a respectful nod.

"I assume you're here to reactivate the portal? I've never attempted this sort of thing. Forgive me if it takes a few tries..."

Elliot gave her a nod, I watched as she straightened her spine. With tense focus, the gatekeeper thrust out the palm of her glove toward the inactive portal. She began to delicately pluck the air with her fingers as if she were drawing string from a loom. She lifted her other gauntlet high in the air, then down to the first—weaving something invisible and small within her metallic hands.

"It looks fascinating, doesn't it?" Elliott whispered into my ear. "I enjoy watching her work. She's playing an instrument we cannot see or hear, and yet... you can *feel* the magic, can't you?"

I *could* feel it. There was power in this place beyond anything I'd ever witnessed. My fingertips instinctively went to my neck, pressing lightly against the amulet that hung there. It felt warm to the touch.

Twisting her stance and rapidly whirling her hands in a powerful arc, the gatekeeper took a step towards the massive metal arch, quickly rolled her arms before thrusting out both palms with a snarl. Her efforts paid off, as the arch immediately began to tremble. I gasped as the air between it glowed once, then twice, engulfing the room in a devilish flash of light. The chrysm under the glass floor began to churn, and the portal roared to life before us.

The polite, gratified gatekeeper smiled in triumph and turned to us all.

"Lords Craven... the portal awaits."

"Excellent. You are dismissed."

Even with the thick visor covering most of her face, the gatekeeper looked surprised. "Lord Craven, are the others... *staying* at the castle?"

"The vampire lords wished to see the chrysm portal reactivated," he crossed his arms wearily as the others merely looked amused. "They will be our guests, and they are welcome to leave at their pleasure."

"*Or their displeasure,*" Nikki muttered under her breath, just barely loud enough for me to hear. I glanced at her long enough to catch a wicked smile fading from her lips.

☙❧

THE VAMPIRE LORDS FOLLOWED ALONG AS THE CRAVENS escorted us all to a vacant tower above the castle bailey. Standing diagonally across the bailey from Craven Keep, it was shorter but no less imposing.

"This tower is normally unoccupied," Elliott explained in fatigue. "Each floor is a private domicile you should find suitable for your stay in Stonehold. Please forgive the lack of servants. In the morning, I will have quality stewards assigned to tend to your every need. In the meantime, I will leave royal guards posted at the entrance to the tower.

"Does this mean we are prisoners or guests?" Lord Vasiliev asked.

"They are there for our *mutual* protection, but you have my word that they will do you no harm. If you wish to leave the castle at any time, they will accompany you to the portal chamber," Elliot replied quietly.

"We appreciate your hospitality, Lord Elliott," Eyes-Like-Fire smiled warmly. "I'm sure this will do."

A few of the others cast her a look, but said nothing.

"Who gets the spire?" Svetlana asked, glancing up the imposing tower.

"Perhaps you should fight for it," Nikki grinned.

Elliott and I gave her a look, but half the lords laughed at her indiscretion. "Your obligations are over, Lord Elliott," Lord Vasiliev dismissed us. "Get your rest. After breakfast, we expect to discuss the fate of your human—and of Stonehold."

Whether or not it was meant to be a threat, it hung in the air like one. The vampire lords bid us good night, each of them stopping to greet me one last time.

Lord Blackburn stayed until last.

"I wish to speak with Lorelei before I go," he spoke.

"Why?" Elliott asked.

Before the lord could answer, Nikki shrugged. "When we thought the vampire lords were going to destroy this castle, Lord Blackburn *only* one standing on our side. Far as I'm concerned, he can do whatever he likes without an inquisition..."

"That is generous of you," he bowed his head.

"Yeah, well... *I'll* still be escorting you. I might be generous, but I'm no fool. I'll take you where you need to go within the castle," Nikki continued.

For a moment, I thought I saw the lord smile.

"Of course," he replied sagely. "Even among your allies, Nikki Craven, there is no reason to let down your guard. I'd have considered you a foolish and vulnerable lord to demand anything less."

Nikki grinned sadistically—I'd actually *missed* that evil little glint in her eye. "Lord Blackburn, I am alive today because I am neither of those things."

"Of course," he replied, amused. "I believe I understand your true nature."

Elliott's sister smiled her darkest. "If *that* is true, you're a fool to stand so close to me."

The lord didn't look even remotely fazed; instead, he politely bowed his head without any attempt to move away. "Sincerest apologies."

Nikki sharply turned to her brother. "Are you going to stop me, oh mighty Lord of Stonehold? I don't see a reason to deny Lord Blackburn his request, but speak now or *forever* hold your peace..."

"Do as you wish," Elliott replied dryly.

"You heard the man," Nikki smirked. "Off we go!"

Lord Blackburn followed her, but not before casting me a small, interested glance. Of all the vampire lords at the table, he had been one of the most fascinating, not least because he was waiting at the castle when we made our journey back between the worlds.

I wonder what his place in all of this was.

"So, what now?" I asked Elliott. "Are we free to go?"

"I think so," he noted. "Nikki and Lorelei can handle anything Lord Blackburn might be cooking up, and the others are retiring to their chamber. This has been a truly overwhelming day. What I need now more than anything is sleep…"

That might be the first time I've agreed with you since we got here—not that you need to know that...

Thanks to the castle's magical teleportation nodes, it wasn't long before we'd blinked into his private suite from across the stronghold. Resting atop Craven Keep, the rooms were largely how I remembered them, although it felt like I'd been gone from this place for an eternity. They were lavish, regal, and befitting a man such as Elliot…

Once we stepped off of the node into his chambers, I tried to hide my growing contempt by reacquainting myself with them. I knew the first thing I wanted to see, and so I pushed my way to his balcony and leaned over the stone railing.

That magical sky awaited me.

I heard his voice. "Is it everything you were hoping for?"

Don't ruin this for me, Elliott... It wasn't lost on me that I'd spent the entire year deeply depressed by our separation, only to question my feelings as soon as I arrived here.

Certainly, Kinsey had sewn the seeds of doubt—but they couldn't have lasted on their own. It was Wilhelm's confession that pushed me to take her words seriously. In my absence, Elliot Craven had taken to punishing all who reminded him of me. The worst part was that I could *see* it, especially in the way he confronted Kinsey. The very thought of his anger drove an uncomfortable wedge down into my mind, but I wasn't willing to confront him yet.

I can't blame myself for what happened here—nor will I.

"Clara?" He asked, stepping outside with me.

The words came tersely. "Give me a minute."

"Okay." His voice sounded disappointed, but he honoured my wishes. I felt his presence quietly retreat into the suite, leaving me alone with the stars.

Even the collective threat of the vampire lords here on the Isle of Obsidian did little to stop me from appreciating those gorgeous stars.

They looked just as beautiful as I'd remembered. It felt like... *home.*

*One year. One full, unending year without you in my life, and now that I've gotten you back... I don't know what to do **with** you...* To my annoyance, I couldn't be sure if I was thinking of the stars, or of Elliott Craven.

I'm not certain how much time passed. But, when I wandered back into the suite, I saw to my confusion and frank relief that Elliott was nowhere to be seen.

Disrobing, I slowly climbed into his massive bed and settled down on my own side. It felt both comforting and alienating to be here alone.

I cried myself to sleep.

CHAPTER 7

LORELEI

My gaze quietly drifted over the courtyard garden. This place brought me a great deal of peace. It was a beautiful array of endless flowers, even with the frost in the air that chilled the petals to glass.

I wondered who planted all of this.

It seemed melancholy.

My battle in this courtyard felt like a distant dream, both to the environment and to me. It was a part of the past, or perhaps it never happened at all.

I sensed the presence of another.

"Lorelei…"

Lorelei, I thought. *What a beautiful name.*

"You are…" I looked up. A handsome face wandered over and sat down beside me, resting on the edge of the courtyard platform. When he looked into my eyes, his gaze was heartbroken. "Do I know you?"

"No," he looked away. "Of course you don't."

We sat in silence together for a while.

"These are beautiful," I finally spoke.

"The gardens?"

"Yes. Were they always like this?"

"No," he noted sadly. I wondered why he was sad. "Someone planted each flower with her own bare hands. It was an act of love."

"That must have taken forever."

"It took decades. She could have used magic to spring these gardens in a week, but she chose a more personal touch." He sighed heavily. "You can feel her touch in every inch of the soil."

"Maybe that's why I like it…"

"The love?"

"Yes."

"I know."

I think I quite liked this man. He had a strong presence. I felt safe near him, somehow, like he was familiar and kind.

"Why were they planted?" I asked. "Decoration?"

"It's a memorial."

"A memorial? She must have been positively heartbroken." I quietly reflected on that for a moment. "Who died?"

"Her eldest daughter."

I felt a pang of recollection, but it faded as quickly as it arrived. It seemed like a fleeting moment of sympathy, but that didn't feel quite right. Before I could reflect on it, I'd lost the feeling entirely.

"Her daughter was her entire world. I don't think she ever healed from that loss. Three centuries of life, snuffed out in an instant…"

Three centuries? Is that… long?

It didn't feel quite right to ask.

There was something I knew I should say, but I couldn't find the words. The complicated fragments of my thoughts confused me; they spiraled like snowflakes out of my grasp, before my fingers could grace them. It made me afraid, or saddened, or disinterested. I couldn't tell anymore, and there was a peace in that.

"I don't know how I came to be here," I told him.

He swallowed; a tear slid down his cheek. I wanted to reach over and brush it away—but I didn't know if it was inappropriate for me to do so.

"You overexerted yourself, Lorelei. The fight took away what little strength you held tightly, and there is nothing left to restrain the curse." The man glanced away. The expression on his face made me want to console him, but I wasn't sure how I could. "It was only a matter of time, but I hoped you would hold on a bit longer…"

I nodded. "There was a fight?"

The man glanced at me with pity, or was it sorrow? Emotions were so hard to read. "Yes. You fought."

"Did I win?"

"You won."

"What did I win?"

"The protection of those who matter most."

I was disappointed. "I'd rather win a thicker robe and a warm fire…"

The handsome man smiled. "Even as you fade away from me, my beloved Lorelei, you never cease to make me laugh."

"You didn't laugh, though."

"No." He looked elsewhere. "I guess I didn't."

A few moments passed as I stared at the gardens.

"I want to see more of them."

"The ones who matter most?"

I glanced towards him. *How long has he been here? Was he **always** this handsome?* "No," I replied. "The gardens."

He nodded distantly. "Okay."

Rising from my seat, I began walking towards the nearest hedges. As I drew closer, I found the crystalline flowers were even more beautiful against the snow than I could have imagined. They felt important, in a way. It was hard for me to tell, but they filled me with, well... *something* that I felt I was supposed to feel. I loved them.

I looked over my shoulder. "Aren't you coming?"

The man glanced up at me. "Do you want me to?"

I thought about telling the man that I thought he was handsome; I wanted to ask him if his heart belonged to another. He radiated such strong love, like these gardens did. I wanted him to understand that he deserved to feel wanted and adored—but to do such a thing didn't feel proper... even if I wanted nothing more than to know the answers.

Instead, I shrugged.

He followed after me.

I nearly smiled.

Together, we strolled into the myriad rows of frozen flowers. We walked past the widest assortment of natural beauty I think I've ever laid eyes upon. It felt magical to witness the splendor of this place, even if I didn't understand what it was, or how it'd come to be. Within this testament to nature we spent an hour, or a thousand years, or twenty minutes—I lost track of the passage of time. Eventually, we crossed a small bridge, deep within a large clearing in the gardens. I looked over the hedges to see a magnificent castle.

I wondered who lived there.

"I am tired," I told the stranger.

"We can rest for a minute if you'd like."

I nodded wearily. "Thank you."

We sat down together on a small bench.

The side of my head slumped against his shoulder. I didn't mean to do that—it wasn't proper—but he struck me as someone who wouldn't mind. Whoever he was, he didn't move me or tell me to stop. In fact, his arm slid around my other shoulder, and I felt warmed by his presence.

"How long have we been in this place?" I asked.

"As long as I can remember."

"Oh."

I lifted my eyes to the stars, twinkling in the night sky against a vortex of cosmic colours. The moonlight poured down, bathing these gardens in a beautiful glow. The view made for a spectacular array of light, blending the best that the horizon could offer.

I stared up at those beautiful stars thinking that I should recognize their arrangement. They shimmered down upon us like the gateway to something beyond, and I took a deep breath.

In that moment, everything felt right.

"I love you, Lorelei Craven," the stranger whispered to somebody. "You are *everything* to me, my dearly beloved."

I nodded faintly.

For some reason, I wished he were talking to me.

The stars continued to twinkle above us. Somehow the colours of the sky looked different.

"How should we sit here?"

"Forever."

"That seems long. Are you uncomfortable?"

"No. This is right where I want to be."

I broke into a smile; I didn't know why. Some distant part of me was pleased to hear his words, for a reason that was beyond me.

"I think this is where I want to be, too," I replied.

"Good," he swallowed.

"I can't keep my eyes open."

He nodded sadly. "Sleep, my beloved Lorelei."

I thought I heard him crying. I wanted to console him, but I felt too tired. *He'll be fine without me,* I thought. *This warm and handsome man...*

I closed my eyes for the final time.

And this beautiful world faded away.

CHAPTER 8
NIKKI

I was practicing my dagger play—hurling them in an arc against the midnight sky, pelting wooden targets easily fifty meters away when I felt it.

The blade in my hand clattered against the stone.

It was an intense emotional rush: complicated and overwhelming. It was so blisteringly strong in my head that it washed away my choking insanity, even if only for a little while, like a scrubbing wave of soothing soap. Steeling myself with a palm against the side of the castle bailey hut, I felt a new surge now: stinging tears, welling up against my eyes.

They say that the vampire lords are connected—it's in the blood, tying them all together. When one passes, the rest of them *feel* it. Nobody knows how or why, and with lives as long as ours, it's not a common thing to experience. The stories say it has something to do with the Sanguine Ones, our fabled predecessors. My resistance to undergoing the Ascension meant that I never thought I'd have to experience this for myself...

Another brief burst in my head, like a wave…

It was weaker this time—but at least it pointed me in the direction where I'd left Mattias. Lorelei had insisted on privacy in the gardens, but I never expected this.

I pulled myself together and retrieved my daggers. If Mattias were responsible for this feeling, I was going to show him pain like he could only imagine.

I would enjoy that quite a bit…

⚜

THE BURST IN MY HEAD CAME TWICE MORE, AND EVER FAINTER. It led me to the only place that made sense.

I found them in the center of the gardens.

Lord Blackburn was seated on a bench. In his lap, he cradled my mother's head, stroking her hair as he stared without seeing. He didn't even notice me arrive.

A moment later, my brother was at my side. He looked exhausted—like he'd just climbed out of bed and rushed straight here from atop Craven Keep.

"Mattias?" His weary voice sounded alarmed.

The lord vaguely turned our way. "Yes?"

"What happened?"

Lord Blackburn looked down at her. "She wanted to walk in these gardens one last time, before she…" He coldly averted his eyes.

"Get up," Elliott growled tiredly.

Mattias nodded. He carefully lowered her head back down to the bench and stood.

The chill we felt had nothing to do with the frost.

Elliott was at a loss. We both were… but deep down, I

knew the truth. Mattias wasn't responsible for this moment of intense pain.

"Lorelei... *Mother, I...*"

In a burst of activity, we weren't alone.

One by one, the other vampire lords arrived at our side— half of them looked like they had just been roused from bed. *I suppose they* **were**...

"No," Svetlana whispered.

Lord Vasiliev glared towards my brother, a crushed look on her face. *I never recalled her being very friendly to Mum... why would she take this to heart now?* "What is the meaning of this?"

"We found her like this," he replied coldly.

The vampire lords scrutinized us carefully. Clearly, there were questions to be asked... not that I blamed them. Vampire lords were not particularly known for just dropping dead in their prime.

They're already beginning to suspect the worst. Isn't that grand?

"Lorelei Craven is one of the greatest vampire lords to ever walk this world," the characteristically stoic and dispassionate lord of The Drenchlands snarled furiously.

"*Arguably,*" Lord Vasiliev dryly added.

Lord Lovrić snapped. "My friend did not *merely* keel over and die. She had not reached her final equinox!"

"True." Lord Krum gravely shook his head with a despairing expression in his somber eyes. It was easy to read him, for once. "This has all become too much."

"But... how?" Lord Eyes-Like-Fire repeated quietly. "How could've this happened? Was she sick?"

"Perhaps it was Lord Azuzi," Lord Song guessed.

"That is a *dangerous* accusation," the eldest of us growled angrily. "How could he have possibly killed her from within the dungeons?"

"Maybe his weapon was poisoned?"

"This discussion will bring us *nothing!*" Elliot shouted, silencing the assembled lords. "If this were an act of violence, we would *know*. We would feel it in every part of our body. My mother is at peace, and I will not tolerate wild speculation in these gardens."

I sensed Elliott beginning to snap. The realization suddenly struck me like a freezing bucket of iced water: *he can't handle this anymore. This single evening has been one swerving disaster after another—he can't keep this up. Elliott's already at his limit...*

I resisted the sudden urge to push him over the cliff of insanity. Instead, I wrapped an arm around my brother and pulled him close. He sighed darkly under his breath. "Will this day never end?"

"We have seen this with our own eyes," Mattias suggested sternly, "I feel that we should leave the Cravens to deal with their loss…"

The other lords nodded gravely. One by one, they turned to offer us a fleeting glance of condolence… while barely hiding their suspicion. With that, then they were gone.

All but *one*.

Lord Blackburn stared at our mother with a bitter look of despondence. "I will grant you privacy as well, young Cravens. When you're both ready, I wish to meet with you in the castle study…"

"No," Elliott replied. "Not tonight."

He blinked. The lord thought on that for a moment, and he nodded. "Of course. Forgive me. You need time." While giving a curiously lingering look over our mother on the bench, Lord Blackburn breathed deeply. "We do have things to discuss, separately from the other lords—I'd hoped to take your ear before they arrived at the castle."

"That opportunity has since passed," Elliott noted.

"Maybe—but it is of paramount nature. Bleakwood is the final hold that Lorelei Craven approached. She has told me a great deal of things that I suspect she wanted you to know. We should speak at length *before* the others reconvene—"

Elliott was a ball of barely contained rage. Before he could turn to Mattias and burn down this bridge, I glared at the lord.

"With all due respect, Lord Blackburn—if you don't leave us now, your intestines shall become my personal *play-thing...*"

Mattias paused. "That is quite a threat."

I smirked, turning to him. "One that I am quite capable of following through with. Look in my eyes and tell me that you don't believe me."

"Fine," he sighed. "Know that you're making a mistake. You will find yourself grossly uninformed when it is time to meet in the morning..."

"We'll manage," Elliott snapped.

Mattias walked past us. The lord paused briefly, as if to say something else, but he shook his head and left.

When we were alone, I turned to Elliott. My brother held his clenched fists at his sides as he held his gaze on our mother's peaceful body. As cold as I knew he could be, I recognized he was on the verge of tears.

I uncoiled his hand and threaded our fingers. He broke his gaze and looked at me, and I am sure I stared at him with the same shattered expression. The evidence was right in front of us, but I barely believed the truth.

"She's gone," I whispered.

He nodded distantly.

"I thought we had more time."

Reluctantly—knowing that every step brought me closer to acceptance, I brought him to the bench. We stood over Lorelei Craven, comprehending a loss I'd felt only once before... with my sister...

"She told me Fiona was buried here," he said. "This will be mother's final resting place. It's where she would have wanted to be..."

It was the first time since returning to the island, that I'd heard him call her that in less than a mildly scathing tone. I don't know why it surprised me, but it did.

"I guess it's fitting..."

"Let us make a pact," he swallowed.

I was grateful that the whispers in my head were silent.

"What kind of *pact*?"

My brother looked at me the way he used to, when we were still innocent children—before my magic twisted my mind. I missed this simple connection, deep down, and it took a moment of lucidity to remind me of all the little things I'd lost.

I knew what he meant, even though he couldn't say it. *I* couldn't bring myself to say it either. In the absence of mum, we would tackle the dangers of this world together... no matter the cost or the consequence. He needed a bond that runs *deeper* than blood. Taking a deep breath as we stared down at the our mother, I quietly nodded.

"Okay."

CHAPTER 9
CLARA

W hen I awoke early the next morning, I didn't recognize the ceiling above my head. For the first few moments, I groggily stared up at it until the pieces finally clicked.

I'm back! My eyes flew wide open.

I was quicker to recognize that my recurring nightmare hadn't come.

Looking to my side, I noticed Elliott Craven's form splayed out across the bed.

He's still dressed in the clothes I gave him...

A goofy smile spread across my face as I started to move towards him, but that's when the cold memories of the night came drifting back...

For a second, I really thought that I could ignore the things Wilhelm and Kinsey had told me... but I couldn't reconcile how much Elliott had clearly changed. Their confessions stole away some of the joy in my heart.

I wiped away a tear from my eyes and sat up in bed. It was

rare to awaken and find Elliott still asleep. He was usually gone by sunrise, off tending to his hold. Speaking of, a glance towards the window showed that the dawning sun was only just cresting above the horizon.

I wouldn't have much time to myself.

Carefully, I rose from the bed. As a painful twist of thoughtfulness, Elliott had seen fit to set a folded pile of fresh clothing out for me; the sight of them dug away at my conviction.

Scooping up the clothes, I cast him a sorrowful eye and quietly let myself out of his bedroom.

⚜

I REMEMBERED WHAT IT WAS LIKE TO BE HERE BEFORE—AT THE very beginning. Elliott Craven had kept me locked up at the top of his private tower to protect me from all of the other vampires in his castle.

It had been a worthy concern. The *one time* that an untreated vampire was in a room with me, it nearly cost me my life…

But that was a distant fragment of the past, thanks to the protection spell cast upon me. The spell seemed to endure traveling between our worlds. I was just as free as ever to roam the castle without the fear of instant destruction—at the hands of a bloodthirsty and uncontrollable vampire…

Unfortunately, the portals required the access of a Craven, so that meant taking the stairs.

*Luckily, **down** is easier than **up**…*

Ten minutes later, I pushed my way out of Craven Keep and into the rising sunlight over the horizon. Even with the stars still twinkling far above, I had to briefly shield my eyes from the brightness.

"Greetings, Clara Blackwell."

I turned. A pair of royal guards stood stationed near the entrance, straightening at attention.

"Good morning," I smiled weakly. "Why are the two of you here? I don't remember the tower getting its own guards at the door."

"Lord Elliott requested guards at every post," one of them told me. "He expects full safety and observation of the royal guest…"

"Me," I sighed.

"Exactly," said the other.

"Right. Well, I don't need a chaperone."

"You must be accompanied by at *least* two guards."

"But neither of you can do it, right?"

They shared a look. "We can."

"No, somebody's gotta watch the door."

"That's… true," the first one noted.

"It's fine. I have a solution."

"Going back inside?" The other cheerfully asked.

"Not a chance," I smirked. "I'll stay here with one of you, but I want the *other* to go find a replacement group of guards. I have a particular three in mind, and I *know* that they're all here somewhere…"

"Oh no," the second shook his head. "Not a chance."

"Why not?"

"Lord Elliott forbade it."

I folded my arms defiantly. "And?"

"He is… our master," the first replied awkwardly.

"It seems there was a *new* vampire lord put into power

while he was gone," I smirked slyly. "Did *Nikki Craven* give up her throne yet? Has she given you any restrictions on who I can and can not see in the castle?"

They shared a confused look.

"Not *precisely*..."

"Then I don't see the problem."

"I'm not sure Lord Craven would—"

I sighed in exasperation. "Don't fight me on this."

The guards turned away in frustration.

"If Elliott Craven punishes you over a request that I gave you, then he will prove right every suspicion I have about the man," I replied furiously. "Now bring me my friends..."

⚘

FIFTEEN MINUTES LATER, THE ROYAL GUARD RETURNED WITH MY beloved Knightly Trio in tow. I visibly lit up as I watched them come out from a nearby door in the castle walls— Wilhelm, Viktor, and Asarra.

"Clara," Viktor replied in a low, serious tone. "We were ordered not to—"

"Don't give me that," I chided him.

"I am delighted," Asarra noted. "But this is unwise."

I turned to Wilhelm. "Do *you* have an opinion?"

He shrugged. "What's *another* rule broken? Until Lord Elliot has me executed, I'm *technically* winning!"

The other two just sighed.

I started wandering across the castle bailey, and the trio fell into step around me. Asarra turned to me with a quiet glance. "So, now that you have returned, what do you want to do first?"

A smile spread across my face. "What's there to do? Anything fun and exciting?"

They glanced among themselves searchingly.

"I do not know," Viktor finally answered. "We have not been on the Isle of Obsidian in some time now. I think we're at a loss here..."

I smiled. "I was here a few days ago..."

Wilhelm blinked. "What?"

"I tried to come back almost a week ago, but it didn't quite work—at least, not in the way I expected."

Asarra tilted her head curiously. Her question came in that delightfully foreign, Slavic accent that I'd missed so much. "What happened, Clara?"

"I might've... *accidentally* kidnapped Elliott and pulled him back to my own world."

The three of them paused in an instant.

"And that's how Nikki ends up in his big fancy chair?" Viktor awkwardly chuckled.

"I guess so..." I smiled nervously. "I had to hide Elliot in my house, away from the rest of the Earth. Between keeping him from feeding on every human in the area and protecting him from the sunlight, I'm not certain I could have managed another day with him..."

"Did you just say *sunlight?*" Wilhelm asked, holding back laughter. "What, was he allergic or something?"

"He might be mad if I tell you."

"Lord Elliott's already going to be furious with us," Viktor wryly observed with a despondent shrug.

Wilhelm nodded. "Might as well even the odds."

I hesitated, glancing between them. "You recall how I told you that the sky is a lot different on my world, right?"

"That rings a bell."

"Yeah, well… the *sunlight* there, I guess it's different too— either that, or the magic in this world protects you from it."

"I do not have magic," Asarra replied.

"No, I don't mean you cast a spell or whatever," I tried to clarify. "I mean the natural magic in your blood. The magic that flows all around us here. Where I come from, none of that exists."

"So the sunlight on your world…?" Viktor asked.

"It *kills* vampires."

Wilhelm sputtered. "Uh, try that one again?"

"The light burns. Elliott touched sunlight for a few seconds fully dressed, and it was enough to scar his hands and cover his body in horrific burns. Oh my god, it was awful to see. He confessed to me that he'd never felt that weak and powerless before…"

"But he's a *vampire lord*," Viktor audibly choked on the words.

Asarra nodded sadly. "The vampire lords—they are meant to be nearly *invulnerable*. You're telling us your world can kill with nothing but light?"

"It's not just that—there is plenty of folklore about vampires on my world. Some of it is pretty insane. I think there's a whole lot of stuff on my Earth that can hurt or kill you guys."

"Oh," Viktor swallowed. "I see."

"Lord Elliot didn't *look* burned," Asarra noticed.

"Yeah!" Wilhelm nodded. "Did he heal up?"

"Not immediately," I confessed.

"But he *could* heal it," Viktor smiled. "Good."

"Not by himself."

They shared a look. Asarra narrowed her eyes; she turned to me accusingly. "What aren't you telling us?"

"I had to feed him," I replied meekly.

"You let him... *feed* on you?" Viktor blinked.

"I didn't let him bite me. It was the only way! He wasn't getting better and I *had* to save him. Elliott looked so pitiful, covered in all those burns and sulking in my chair. He wasn't himself—he'd turned into some vulnerable, terrified husk..."

"That is horrifying," Asarra observed fearfully.

"Well, so much for my *vacation!*" Wilhelm snorted. "You know, they don't tell you this stuff when they get you to sign up. Guess I'd better unpack my suitcase..."

۞

WE STAYED IN THE BAILEY, OBSERVING THE EARLIEST OF THE vampires of the little village as they staggered outside for work. It didn't seem that they noticed me at first. One of the blacksmiths eventually glanced our way and froze on the spot. I waved, just to be polite. He immediately turned and walked straight back into his house.

I didn't mean to interfere—I just wanted to watch.

"Perhaps we should leave," Viktor whispered.

I was about to agree when the blacksmith came out again, carrying a young vampire child against his side. He looked at me with a curious glance; his gaze drifted up to the rooftop of Craven Keep.

"He's afraid," Wilhelm replied. "None of them have really ever interacted with you, have they?"

Viktor folded his arms with an amused expression. "They knew Lord Elliott disappeared—and I suspect they believe *you* were responsible for that. It may surprise them to see you here, as I doubt the news of Elliot's return has spread through the village this early in the day…"

"Enough is enough," I decided.

I strolled towards the blacksmith and his daughter. The young girl looked at me with a beaming grin on her face, but her father took a defensive step backward.

"It's okay," I told him. "I won't hurt you."

"*You* are not who I fear," he replied in gravelly tone. "It is the lord of the castle who concerns me…"

I sighed. *Just more evidence that Elliott hasn't been at his best in my absence.*

"Forget about him."

The blacksmith laughed. "That's easy for you to say…"

The child on his side reached out to me.

"Stop that," he chided her.

"No, really. It's okay."

"Are you… sure?" He looked concerned.

"Of course," I smiled. "May I hold her?"

The blacksmith gazed at his young daughter. "Don't hurt her."

"I really wouldn't worry about any of that if I were you. Humans are remarkably fragile things. Your daughter might already be stronger than I'll ever be."

"Is that so?" He handed her over carefully.

The Knightly Trio watched hesitantly as I took his daughter and held her on my hip, as he'd done. She held up her hands for my hair.

The blacksmith panicked. "Wait! Don't—"

I bobbed my head away before she could rip any of it out. "You don't want to make me cry, do you?"

The child hesitated and shook her head.

"I'm very weak," I smiled. "You're big and strong. If you do that, you'll rip out my hair and hurt me." I cooed at her. "You don't want to *hurt me*, do you?"

The girl put her thumb up to her mouth. "Nuh-uh."

"That's what I thought." I bounced her on my hip as I turned to the blacksmith, growing aware that a crowd was forming around us. "What's her name?"

"Aleric," he replied in awe, watching me hold her.

"And yours?"

"Harken."

"Well, Harken... what were you about to do before I so rudely interrupted?"

"Breakfast," he replied with a smile. "Once a week, we like to eat together as a village—for solidarity."

My stomach grumbled.

"Would you... like to join us?" He asked hesitantly.

"Only if there's room for four more," I glanced over my shoulder at the Knightly Trio—who I realized were covertly trying to motion for me to stop. "I have to keep my friends with me, but I don't want to put you out if there isn't enough for all of us... we can help you cook."

"Nonsense!" An elderly vampire woman cackled. "In nearly nine hundred years, I never thought I'd break bread with a *human!* Oh, if only Mother could see me now! I wouldn't let her hear the end of it!"

The rest of them seemed almost as excited.

I turned to my friends with a big grin.

"Hungry?"

CHAPTER 10
ELLIOTT

I awoke from a plague of horrible dreams.

I couldn't remember anything beyond vague whispers, but they felt like none I had ever experienced. Lying in bed staring up at the ceiling, I tried to make some fleeting sense of them. Eventually, I turned to my right and noticed the bed. I sighed wearily. *Something's gotten into that girl. She's been emotionally distant, ever since last night...*

The memories resurfaced.

The battle between lords in the courtyard...

Akachi's comatose body, in the dungeon...

Lorelei's death in the gardens...

I swallowed in regret and tightly clenched my eyes shut, hoping to block out the painful reminders—but that gave me nothing else to concentrate on.

Well, that—and the fact that I would soon face the vampire lords again. They *had* been surprisingly cordial last night, but I knew today would be far more dangerous. Nothing raised tensions like the death of a vampire lord... and there was something else eating at the edge of my awareness that I couldn't quite put my finger on.

They are up to something... but what?

The day was now rising without me. I climbed up out of my bed and staggered over to the royal closet. *If nothing else, I can finally shed these human clothes for garments more befitting of a vampire lord...*

I paused.

There seemed to be so much to reconcile.

One memory settled at the forefront of my mind, the words Mattias Blackburn had spoken as he took his leave.

I hadn't determined his role in any of this, but he was the last person to see my mother alive.

A painful sting struck my heart as I hesitated in the closet, thinking back on Lorelei Craven. She might have been a thorn in my side—increasingly unreliable, all but personally sabotaging my reign with her complete lack of oversight, training, or assistance in Stonehold—but she was my mother... and it had become clear that she was working behind the scenes to save us all.

And now she was gone, centuries before her time.

Nikki and I were alone in this world now—and she came with her *own* set of complicated problems, not the least of which was her current status as the technical ruler of this hold. I didn't really know how to fix that little problem, so I considered asking for advice from others in the castle.

I cleaned myself up in the bathroom and wandered to the balcony, dressed in proper regal attire. I thought I might enjoy some of this morning sun before I decided to hunt down Clara and get to the bottom of her strange, almost antago-nistic behaviour. Even so, I was careful to allow the light to touch my exposed fingertip before I willingly bathed myself in it.

How long will I fear the light?

As I glanced upon Stonehold Castle, my gaze happened to drift down to the castle village, where I noticed my subjects enjoying a communal meal. Lazily casting them an idle glance I wondered if this was a common occurrence...

My throat choked when I saw Clara among them—and worse still, her Knightly Trio sitting around her.

I felt my blood boil in my veins.

Before I realized what I was doing, I lunged from the balcony and descended rapidly towards the village. With the coursing strength of vampire lord blood in my veins, I was unconcerned with the ground rushing up from below...

Some of the villagers noticed me before my boots crashed against the earth. A large burst of snow kicked up in my wake as I rose to my feet.

"Lord Craven! You have returned!"

The merriment at the feast vanished almost as quickly as I had arrived. My voice growled with seething and unfathomable rage.

"I believe I made myself *very* clear..."

"Elliott, don't."

My eyes narrowed upon Clara Blackwell. "You *think* you know what you're doing, but don't intervene. You have always been blind to their incompetence."

She rose from the table in defiance.

"These are my friends, and *you* will leave them be."

"Your *friends* have failed to protect you," I countered angrily. "They add *insubordination* to their many flaws. I gave them explicit instructions—"

"Which I overruled," she folded her arms.

"You do not have that power."

Clara scoffed. "I can do as I please, Elliott. I am not one of your *subjects*."

I seethed—and I felt powerless. It was the same sort of feeling that overcame me when her world viciously burned my body. I couldn't help but find myself associating the two sensations with the lowest common denominator.

Clara...

My head shook. *No. Don't think like that.*

"You don't understand," I responded coolly. "Please calm down and listen to reason."

"Calm down? How do you expect me to *calm down?*" She stamped her foot in the ground. "Everybody in this castle—your subjects, your guards, your own *vassals*—they tell me the same thing. They say you've *changed* since I left. They say you've gotten worse. They all tell me that you are becoming a tyrant..." She briefly hesitated, studying me at a glance.

I recalled who first used that word against me.

Kinsey, I snarled inwardly. *What did you do...?*

The situation needed to be defused, and fast. "This *isn't* the time, Clara. Let us talk in private before we reconvene with the other lords..."

"No," she shook her head.

"Clara..." I felt a knife twist in my heart.

"I *know* what you did to my friends. None of this was their fault! If *anyone* was to blame for what happened to me, it would be Nikki—and don't you *dare* try to think up some new way of punishing *her*."

I groaned, wondering what Lorelei might advise me to do —if she were alive...

*Don't reopen **that** wound right now...*

"Listen to me—"

"No, *you* listen to *me*."

"Clara—something's happened. If we could just talk in private, I'll explain everything—"

"You're *not* listening." Clara turned her back on me. "You sent me away from this place against my will, but I was responsible for my return. I am not the powerless girl you remember. I will *not* let you hurt my friends again, and I will *not* let you scare all these people over breakfast."

She had a fire in her eyes that struck me as dangerous. I took notice of the way her hand had instinctively reached up to her neck to grasp at her pendant.

"Do you think you can so easily control me? Are you going to send me over to that mine and hand me a spear? Shall I stand guard against the tatzelwurm too, if it comes back?"

My chest froze. I looked to Viktor.

"No," Victor shook his head, responding to a question I didn't even need to ask. "I didn't tell her anyth—"

"I know *everything*," Clara snarled.

I lowered my head. The pain of Lorelei's death kept me sapped of energy—I couldn't find the resolve within me to face her like this, nor did I even want to. *At least it was all starting to make sense, what got into you...*

"I thought we were a team, you and I."

She scoffed, sending me a scathing glare. "We were, Elliott. I thought you were still the man I remembered, but now that I've heard about the things you've done..."

Everyone was silent.

"I am not a monster," I said.

"Then prove it."

My eyes scoured the village. I had never before been so overwhelmed with the desire to destroy them—but they had done nothing to arouse my anger. That particular luxury went to these three, who had been a thorn in my side from the moment that Clara met them.

When Wilhelm and Viktor were first left alone with her, they sent a vampire *straight* to her room—and had I not intervened, he would have *killed* her.

In just a single day, they had turned her against me, and I felt certain this all began with my vassal, *Kinsey*...

Funny how she'd saved my life—only to rip out my heart from my chest.

I did not have the strength to bicker any longer. My heart cold and heavy like a rounded stone in my aching chest, I turned and abandoned them all.

CHAPTER 11
CLARA

The rest of the village had barely spoken to me as we finished the feast—and I wasn't quite sure why. They were happy to take care of the cleanup themselves, even though I'd already offered to help with that part.

As the Knightly Trio led me further into the castle to take a strong look around and get reacquainted, I sensed their looming judgment and the stiffness of the air.

The sun was high in the sky when my friends finally brought me back to the castle gardens. Fondly, I recalled how much Lorelei Craven loved this part of the castle—and the stories of how she'd planted the flowers as a beautiful tribute to her fallen daughter, Fiona.

"It's just as beautiful as I remember," I noted sadly. "Lorelei took me on a walk through these gardens once."

"I remember," Viktor recalled. "We were all on very strict orders not to let you out of our sight, even when it came to the matron of the castle."

"You've always been so good to me, all of you. I don't know what I would have done without you three."

"You might have been a lot safer," Asarra grumbled.

"What do you mean?"

The others grew conspicuously uncomfortable.

"I have told you this once before," the young guard crossed her arms, her stern voice in that foreign accent. "You are much too forgiving, Clara Blackwell, to those who would cause you harm."

"I am not."

"Wilhelm and Viktor almost got you killed."

"Hey now," Wilhelm tried to cut in.

Viktor placed a firm hand on his shoulder. "She is right. Have you so quickly forgotten the tailor?"

"That was an honest mistake!"

"But it *was* a mistake. We got lucky."

Asarra cut them an angry glance, and they quieted down. She turned back to me. "Then there is the sister of Lord Elliott—you think her to be your friend."

"She *is* my friend."

"She incapacitated us and nearly handed you over to Sabine, the traitor from abroad," Asarra's glower slowly melted into a smile.

"And she's *completely* insane," Wilhelm added, laughing.

"And do you remember how *we* met?" Asarra asked.

"You were the first guard to find me," I grinned.

"I *captured* you." She sighed wearily. "Clara, there is a great power in making allies of your enemies—but you take things all too far. Lord Elliot has been far from a perfect ruler, but he understands your biggest flaw. Even if he falters, our master does what he thinks is right. He grows as fast as the world lets him—and he will be a great, in time…"

"You think I went too far," I groaned.

She placed a gloved hand to my forehead, stroking my hair. It was the most tender thing the relatively stoic guard had ever done in front of me—or *to* me. "Elliot suffered greatly."

"He *terrified* his own people," I replied firmly.

"He made strong decisions," she rebutted.

"*Bad* decisions."

"I did not say they were good. Only strong."

"I don't understand."

Viktor spoke up. "I think that what Asarra is trying to tell you is that Stonehold is in crisis—it needed a *strong* leader. Our liege rose up to the challenge and did his best with what information he had on hand. Some of his decisions threaten the long term future of this hold, but the alternative was death and destruction."

"I don't see how you can defend him," I shook my head woefully. "After what he did to you."

"Perhaps we are all trying to take a page out of *your* book," Viktor smiled sympathetically. "You've forgiven us for the ways in which we put your life in danger. You asked us all to be your guardians—something we are all proud to do."

"This is correct," Asarra replied offhandedly.

They looked at Wilhelm.

"It passes the time…"

Amused, I shook my head at him.

"What do you think I should do?" I asked them all.

Wilhelm replied dryly. "When you two were reunited on your world, how was he?"

"Afraid," I replied. "Scared. Wounded."

"Right, the burns," he shuddered. "*Besides* the part where he was in utterly agonizing pain…"

"He was… himself?" I tilted my head, trying to remember the details. "Eager to learn. He was curious about all the little details of my world—even the bad bits."

"The bad bits?"

"I'd tell you all about them, but I don't have any cat videos…" I replied quietly.

"Cat videos?" Wilhelm asked, clearly confused. I just laughed.

"It's an inside joke…"

Asarra nodded. "What else?"

"He was sarcastic," I grinned to myself. "Elliott was a whole lot *snarkier* than I remembered him being."

"But *not* dark and brooding?" Viktor asked.

"Well… no."

"At all?"

"No."

Wilhelm shrugged, a dopey smile on his face. "I'm certain your first impulse is to be angry at him on *everyone* else's behalf—and I can't say I blame you… but antagonizing him in front of his own subjects? That *might not* be the way to go…"

Viktor nodded in agreement. "I saw how he changed around you—and if there is *anything* that could bring that part of him back, I think it's a power that resides with *you*. You have an effect on him that none of us can hope to match, Clara."

Asarra thought for a moment. "He needs your support. This hold lives or dies by the hard decisions Lord Elliot is forced to make. That is why the villagers did not appreciate how you…"

"Intervened?" Wilhelm offered helpfully.

"Yes. How you *intervened*," she continued.

"So… what? Should I just ignore his actions?"

Wilhelm sighed. "Give our liege a real chance to become something more than his actions. Let him take a shot at redemption."

"I didn't think you'd feel so strongly about it."

"We think you both make each other better," Viktor observed. "At least, I do." The others nodded.

"I'm perfect just how I am!" I smiled warmly.

Asarra snorted. "I think not. You halted a breakfast feast to challenge the lord of the castle in front of his own people. You refused to let him get a word in. You drew a line in the sand, forcing him into a corner and humiliating him. No, little Clara, I think you might be a little far from perfect…"

I sighed. "Well, damn…"

They'd given me a lot to think about, even if I didn't quite agree with all of it. *Maybe I **was** in the wrong. Pushing Elliott like that, without even **trying** to talk to him about this might not have been the right choice…*

"Just think about it," Viktor offered. "From the looks of things, your time apart has changed *you* just as much as it's changed him."

"Is it so obvious?" I replied dryly.

"Asarra smiled warmly. "Anyway, you're back. You have all the time you need to find the answers in your heart."

I wish I'd known just how wrong she was.

Time was a precious commodity, and it was quickly running out.

⚜

I⊤ WASN'T LONG BEFORE ANOTHER VAMPIRE ENTERED THE ROOM.

"Miss Clara, your presence has been requested."

I blinked. "Who requested it?"

"Lord Craven," the servant grinned cheerfully. "He was quite insistent."

I shook my head. "He should know better than to push me —I'm not afraid to admit that I'm feeling a bit vulnerable right now. This isn't a good time to 'request' me."

The servant smiled weakly. "Be that as it may, Lord Craven made his intentions explicitly clear. As the royal guest of this castle, you cannot refuse his summons. It's the law of the castle."

"Is that so?" I folded my arms in disgust. "He can't control me himself, so he sends a servant to do retrieve me?"

*To think, I actually almost felt **sorry** for him for a fleeting moment.*

"Elliott can come and get me himself."

The servant's smile faltered. "He cannot."

"Then I guess I'm staying here."

"You don't understand—he is currently—"

"I said *no*," I held my ground. "Tell him that."

Asarra stole my gaze. "Miss Clara—it is *imperative* that you—"

"For the *last time*, tell the *great Lord Elliott* that the next time he wishes to 'request my presence,' he can do so in person."

Sighing wearily, the servant left us.

"I hope you know what you're doing," Viktor noted.

I smirked confidently. "He changed things when he sent me away."

"We have been over that," Asarra reminded me.

"And his idea of defusing the situation is to send a *servant* to come and retrieve me," I snapped irritably. "If he's ready to talk, I'll meet him halfway…"

The others shook their heads, but I didn't care.

How terrible naïve I was.

CHAPTER 12
ELLIOTT

*Clara Blackwell, **how dare you** embarrass me in front of the vampire lords—I'd have come and gotten you myself if they'd let me slip away...*

"I take it she's not coming," Lord Blackburn noted.

"This is why I asked to retrieve her personally," I acknowledged before the others. "You'll have to forgive her. Clara is a woman of strong convictions. I suspected she may react like this if I didn't go to her in person."

"What about your sister?" Eyes-Like-Fire asked. "Is she not the *other* vampire lord of Stonehold?" The tribal lord conspicuously glanced around the room, as if Nikki were hiding in plain sight. "Should she not be here?"

"My sister wishes to be alone," I answered. "She has asked me to speak on her behalf. I'm afraid that I will be the only representation Stonehold has to offer. If you allow me a moment, I will bring the human girl..."

"I think we have all waited long enough," Valentine

Vasiliev replied with obvious contempt. "It was from a place of generosity that I suggested she have a say in her own future. If she's so willing to throw that opportunity away..." Her words ominously trailed off into nothingness.

"She misunderstands the stakes," I countered.

Valentine snorted derisively. "My young lord, that is *not* my problem—nor is it the problem of anyone else at this table. Be it vampire or human, I linger for no one. Clearly she disrespects you, and all of us by extension..." Her stern gaze grew cold and resolute. "So, we shall offer that same courtesy. We continue without her."

Settling back into my chair, I stressfully pressed the fingertips of one hand to my forehead. *Clara... this was **not** the time fight...*

Clearly agreeing with her sentiment, Mattias began the meeting. "It is unusual for us to convene the Council of the Eight Holds away from our sacred place, but this will not be a usual meeting. We must resolve three problems of grave importance. First, we must consider Lorelei Craven's death..." For all his impartiality and stoicism, Lord Blackburn nearly faltered over the words.

Most of the assembled lords nodded in agreement. Of certain curiosity was Svetlana Lovrić, who averted her eyes and stared off into space sadly.

Those two were best friends. Thick as thieves...

"Secondly, there is a traitor in the dungeons below. For now, Lord Azuzi rests placated and restrained—but these are *temporary* measures. We will need to decide the fate of our *misguided* friend."

Valentine Vasiliev hardened her glare, none of the other

lords batted an eye. *Those two were **never** friends... I turned away before she could notice. We are all the better for it. If the two darkest lords among us had only learned to cooperate, they would have forged a deeply formidable alliance...*

"Finally, we must decide what to do with the return of Elliott Craven and Clara Blackwell. Their passage back into this world was no small feat—and there are ramifications to be discussed."

"That's right," Ooktum Krum nodded solemnly. "It is now that we determine what we do with her..."

My attention pricked. "I was under the impression that she was staying here in Stonehold," I replied coldly. "Or has that changed? You all seemed to enjoy her company at the feast..."

"Lorelei Craven is dead," Valentine turned to me. "I speak for myself and none of the others, but her passing changes *everything.* Your mother made deals that you are incapable of honoring in her absence—and I find it a compelling option to withdraw my support."

"What prevents me from honoring those deals?"

She shrugged. "You are *not* Lorelei Craven."

I kept myself from slamming a fist down on the arm of my seat. *This is you abdicating the throne all over, Lorelei. Even in death, you've managed to sabotage me...*

"Let us discuss one thing at a time," Mattias replied in veiled irritation. "While the topic is fresh at hand, it is my suggestion that we start with Lorelei Craven."

"Yes," Chanda Song sadly turned towards me with a small but sympathetic smile. I appreciated the gesture. "What are your plans for the announcement?"

Truthfully, I'd barely even considered that...

"Only Nikki Craven and those of us assembled in this chamber know of my mother's death. It was my intention to discuss the announcement with my high chancellor, Silas. He hails from before her time on the throne, and I believe he would do well in breaking the news to the rest of the castle... and to the mainland."

"Only *we* know?" Eyes-Like-Fire asked with a slight air of curiosity—and the briefest hint of a smirk on her pierced face. "Are we to believe you haven't told your darling Clara of Lorelei's death?"

"Clara has been somewhat *difficult* since our return to Stonehold," I clarified in veiled derision.

"The human sounds difficult to mange," Valentine observed in amusement.

"Perhaps we should all get back to the matter at hand," Svetlana Lovrić cut in with a hint of annoyance. "You plan to speak with your high chancellor—and *then* what, Lord Craven?" She was obviously not pleased with my answer. "Lorelei deserves an appropriate procession."

I restrained irritation. "I am open to suggestions."

"This hold may have special traditions and customs concerning the death of such a figure," Mattias helpfully offered. "I think it is wise that we allow the two Cravens the opportunity to do so as they see fit."

"I want to be involved," Lord Lovrić insisted.

"Let us handle it," I offered diplomatically, aware of how close this must be to her heart. The last thing I needed was one of the lords interfering *further* in my life. "Let me assure you, Lord Lovrić... it will be a fitting funeral."

"That's not good enough."

I set my jaw angrily. "It will have to be."

"As far as I am concerned, this is non-negotiable."

I growled irately toward Lord Svetlana Lovrić, briefly forgetting myself. Under the mounting pressure of her willful insolence, I felt my resolve to merely *survive* this meeting unscathed cracking apart. "I suggest you do not see fit to *blatantly* antagonize me over her lifeless body, especially not within my *own* castle."

Her eyes lit with fury. *"Excuse me?"*

Mattias banged his fist on the table. "Order! My dear Lord Lovrić. The boy has lost his mother. Do not let your emotions pour fuel on the fire!"

She narrowed her eyes. "And what of *your* emotions?"

For once, he was briefly stunned.

"I believe that we should let Lord Craven handle it," Eyes-Like-Fire replied, hoping to ease the tensions. "She was a practical and confident ruler—I'm certain her son will do right by her."

Svetlana set her jaw, but didn't say anything.

"Does anyone disagree with that?" Mattias asked.

The others all shook their heads. Seeing their lack of support, Lord Lovrić rested backwards in her seat in a foul, frustrated air.

"A decision has been made," Mattias simmered. Let us now move on to the matter of Lord Akachi Azuzi…"

⚛

THE LORDS BICKERED OVER *AZUZI* FOR AGES.

I couldn't help but lose focus. With a fist against my cheek, I barely listened to the vampire lords mentally spar over the fate of my greatest enemy.

My mind's preoccupation was with Clara Blackwell. Tragedy and countless obstacles had united us, forging us within the fire of strict opposition. Her very *world* was an utter death trap to me, and my demise was a grave possibility.

*Why must you defy me at every turn? We have **only** just passed the first major hurdle—and I am **still** trying to navigate the murky waters left beyond it.*

Kinsey, I glowered to myself.

My vassal had planted the traitorous seed in Clara's head —but there were three others who helped that seed grow.

What is it with that human and my royal guards? The thought almost made me chuckle sardonically. *It seems like everyone who comes into contact with the human only serves to put her in danger or divide us further...*

I snarled inwardly, feeling the contempt rise within my tired mind.

"Lord Elliott?"

Wearily, I glanced towards the source of the voice. To my quiet consternation, Mattias Blackburn carefully watched me with a solemn expression. "Lord Craven, do you not wish to participate in these talks?"

"Forgive me," I straightened in my seat. "I am tired. have not been given time to properly grieve my mother, and I am still exhausted from my time between worlds. The council is well aware of my frustrations with Lord Azuzi. I did not think that I could offer an... *unbiased* input. I openly and unabashedly consider him to be a thorn in my side..."

"Lord Craven, this is *your* castle," Mattias Blackburn reminded me. "Would you rise to the challenge of keeping Lord Azuzi *contained* here, if that was the decision of the council?"

"You wish to *keep* the lord bound and restrained? Surely the Falvian Badlands would disapprove, and would waste no time empowering his successor. We cannot possibly foresee the full breadth of consequences that might bring upon us..."

Ooktum Krum quietly nodded. "That is a wise observation. What would you suggest we do instead?"

"I am... not entirely certain."

"Come now, young lord," Valentine simmered. "We have been considering your enemy's fate for the greater part of an hour. Have you truly no ideas?"

"He is no friend of mine. Do with him as you wish."

Valentine smirked. "I'm honestly surprised. I might have thought you would take much greater interest in Lord Azuzi's punishment..."

Mattias leaned closer. His neutral gaze stayed calm and collected, but a faint smile lit up on his face. "I see Lord Craven is already focused on Clara's fate."

"You see right through me," I sarcastically noted.

"Then it is settled. For now, Azusi shall remain imprisoned in the dungeons beneath this keep. We shall decide his ultimate fate after we have dealt with matters regarding the human girl."

"Right," Valentine nodded. "Of course."

Eyes-Like-Fire turned towards me with a sly smile. "You appear to have forgotten something, Lord Craven."

"Oh? I wearily asked. "What would that be?"

"The human world," she noted. "We've heard what Clara had to say on what it was like to be back again, but not what *you* learned." She propped up an elbow on the table and planted a fist against her cheek. "Tell me, Lord Craven... what was it like?"

The others turned with unified curiosity.

There's no getting around this, is there...?

"I hope you'll consider my openness with this topic when we discuss Clara's fate. As for her world... it is a beautiful place, *filled* with terrors you could never hope to comprehend."

CHAPTER 13
PETER

"Please," I groaned. "I've been awake for *ages* now."

The man raised his hand to smack me again.

Instinctively, I cowered—but the woman shook her head. Keeping his penetrating gaze firmly locked on me, the man slowly lowered it. I didn't want to let down my guard, but I was exhausted, and I slowly relaxed into the metal seat.

"I think my friend has had enough for now."

I nodded painfully. I hadn't seen a mirror since they shoved me into this holding cell, but my eye was already half-swollen shut, and I could feel the pulsating warmth and string of fresh bruises.

"Why don't you leave us?" She told him from across the table, tilting her head coyly. "We've had a long day, Garrett. Go home. Get some rest. There isn't much more you can do here at the moment..."

"As you wish, Mrs. Partridge."

He gave me a scathing glare and adjusted the cuffs of his fancy dress shirt before leaving the room.

Out of the entire night, it was the first time I'd been left alone with her—I almost wanted him back already. As I felt the inside of my tender jaw with my tongue, the crisp, malevolent woman called Vera Partridge lowered her gaze on me in veiled disapproval.

"Peter," she addressed me coolly, "you haven't been very helpful today. I thought we agreed on that."

I chuckled mirthlessly. "Yeah, well... I'm trying."

"Are you?" She asked, narrowing her eyes.

I remembered, from the moment they captured me at Clara's lake, that she seemed to appreciate honesty. I touched the inside of my swollen cheek with my tongue. *Even when it would logically get me punched...* "You're not really meeting me halfway here."

"Whatever could you mean?"

"You keep asking me questions," I groaned, shifting in my seat. My ribs still hurt from their earlier pounding but I didn't dare check them right now. "But you haven't told me anything. If we're supposed to be *friends...*"

Her eyes widened curiously. "Oh?"

"I don't know who you are. Who *any* of you are."

She smiled. The effect was... *chilling.*

"You raise a valid point, Peter," the woman replied. "What would you like to know?"

"Where... am I?"

"Pass."

I sighed. "Who are you?"

"My name is Vera Partridge."

"Yeah. I gathered that. *Who* are you?"

She tilted her head. "I don't like that tone."

"You'll have to forgive me," I chuckled blearily. It hurt to do that. "I've been having a really bad day…"

Vera leaned back in her chair, clicking her tongue in her parted teeth. She looked away, lost deep in thought. When her eyes snapped back to me, I nearly jumped.

"Fine. I don't see why not…" The woman stared me directly in the eyes with a warm yet calculated gaze. "I am Vera Partridge of Clover Pharmaceutical. My role is the Chief Operations Officer. I serve on the board of directors for international oversight."

"Clover?" I asked, tasting copper in my mouth. "You mean the big international medical corporation, Clover? That one that's always in the news? I've been kidnapped by people who make cold medicine and sleeping pills?"

"You've heard of us," she grinned.

"Oh, I'd be an idiot if I hadn't," I groaned painfully. "Anyone who's turned on a telly or read a newspaper in the past fifteen years has heard of you people. You're one of the biggest corporations on the entire planet. Seems like I can't go a *day* without seeing some advert for yet another cream you make or third-world charity you're spearheading…"

"Our fingerprints are everywhere," she agreed.

"And you *work* for them?"

"As far as you're concerned, Peter, I *am* them."

I took a deep breath. I didn't like the sound of this. "Okay. I'll bite. What interest does a worldwide medical corporation have in, well…?"

"Vampires?" She finished, sweetly.

"Vampires," I swallowed painfully.

"None, really," Vera replied matter-of-factly. "If I'm being perfectly frank with you, I honestly couldn't give a damn if it were a vampire, a werewolf, or some giant *spider* that came crawling out of that rift."

"Then… what are you…?"

"What am I *looking for*, Peter? Is that what you're asking me?" The blank expression across her face was utterly unreadable. "What am I *after*?"

"Sure," I tried to shrug. It hurt too much to do that, so I didn't try it again. "Let's go with that."

Vera pensively bit down on half her lower lip. The other corner pulled up in a smile until she released it all into an amused, curious grin.

"Do you want to hear a story?"

I nodded wearily. "I like stories."

"Get comfortable, then. It's a long one."

By now, there really wasn't anything I could do to *make* myself any more comfortable. I wasn't so inclined to ask her for a fistful of ibuprofen—and especially not one of Clover's top-of-the-line pain pills...

"You already know the bottom half of what I could tell you —you just don't realize it, Peter. You'd heard of vampires *long* before you met one. The fairy tales, the old stories, the super-stitions, the prophecies, the ancient texts… together, they all tell us of a past so many of us have forgotten at best, or fully written off at worst. The facts may have been twisted, but the truth remains. So many of these ancient stories were real, in one shape or another."

Vera paused then, thinking wistfully.

"And how does Clover factor into all of that?"

"Ah, yes. For that, we'll have to turn back the clock. You see, our story starts over a thousand years ago..."

I nearly choked. *You've got to be kidding me.*

"In every major civilization on the planet, for every ruler of every society, there was somebody who claimed to understand and wield magic. Kings, queens, and lords had their own private court wizards; tribal leaders held soothsayers and druids in their ranks. Magic, you see, was a powerful commodity, and it was hard to come by. Great prosperity came to all of those who sought it out and respected it—and those who had the gift."

"You're saying the old myths about magic and sorcery…"

"Yes, Peter. They were real. *Magic* was real. *Folklore* was real. Empires rose and fell based on the powers of magic. Sometimes it was direct—other times, a rising new leader claimed to have had some kind of a powerful vision, and their magnetic ascension was forged with a degree of separation from within the shadows."

"Like Constantine the Great?"

"Excuse me?"

"The man who became Constantine I, who won an impossible war and led the Roman Empire into a new era of religious enlightenment. The old empire fell, but his city stood for centuries. Then along came the Turks, and, well, there's that funny song about Istanbul and Constantinople…"

"You know your history," she noted curiously.

"Yeah, well." I coughed a chuckle. "My teachers are alright, I s'pose. Do love me some history."

"Constantine I claimed to have had a vision before the battle that changed his fate, and the destiny of the Roman Empire. This is one of the many times in history when magic intervened, yes. Magic always played a part in world events— bending the tide of wars, moving and removing families from power, and writing our history books for countless generations. We think it was the cusp of the Middle Ages when the Blackheart Circle was sliding into place. It took more generations than we know for it all to come to fruition. What we *do* know is that a brotherhood drew itself into existence—a silent alliance of black magic practitioners, including powerful members in every civilization, close to every king and every lord. Through careful planning that spanned centuries, the Circle was poised to stand at the ear of every leader of our primitive world... advising individually while secretly ruling collectively, shaping all of history with their unified magic. The Blackheart Circle meant to seize power behind the scenes—in their grand scheme of appointed puppets, shaping the world as their organization saw fit."

"The Blackheart Circle? Guess I must have missed *that* fairy tale," I replied cynically.

"That was the point. No history book in the world knows the name. Their members met in secret, through distant proxies and couriers. The only evidence of their existence is in the archaic tomes that we have now."

"How did you get them?"

"Stop interrupting," she curtly replied. "Unless you simply don't want to hear the rest."

"I'll be quiet."

"Good." She briefly smirked. "But then there came a day when that all of changed. All the magic in our world simply vanished without reason. Overnight, as it were. There was no explanation found, no reason granted—only the loss of power. The ancient texts call it the Cataclysm."

The Cataclysm—I've heard that phrase...

It was easy to hide my horror with a swollen face.

"The Blackheart Circle was finally succeeding in its goals, only to have victory snatched away. Without magic at their ambitious fingertips, the entire brotherhood nearly collapsed. To an extent, it did—the sorcerers blamed one another, splitting up the secret society into warring factions. Anarchy reigned and the world filled with charlatans overnight—those who never dropped their claims of possessing magic, or those who furthermore noticed its sudden unreliability and played that to their own ends. It didn't take long for the work of this organization to fade into oblivion; the magic would never came back, and so the Blackheart Circle became a withered husk of its former self. For all of their previous power, its members rapidly dropped from all the favour they had so carefully cultivated. This is where the Blackheart Circle should've been eradicated from history—but the brotherhood lived on. From the ashes rose the most committed members, once again joined in a dark oath. They endeavored to pursue the same goal with *different* means of attaining it... and to always adapt and survive, never repeating the mistakes of their predecessors. They believed that their mighty hubris had damned them to lose their magic, and the rest of the world as well."

I adjusted in my seat, taking a painful breath as I listened intently.

"And so the remnants of the order were determined to win back the favour of the gods above. If they could not *control* the world with magic, then they would make themselves indispensable to society in *alternative* ways. Power comes in many forms, Peter. Why subvert and corrupt when you can *heal?*"

I didn't like where this was going.

"Generations passed; pestilences came and went. And yet,

the Circle survived, in one form or another. The ancient texts grow in lucidity beyond the Black Plague, in the brotherhood's second or even third iteration. That was their first major test—and they passed, without a single drop of magic at their disposal. At that point, they knew they were on to something."

"What was the test? Creating the Plague?"

"Of course not. The organization had *nothing* to do with that. Our the test was to *stop* the Plague."

"Are you seriously telling me that the descendants of the Blackheart Circle stopped the *Plague?*"

"And so much more than that. Instead of black magic, the brotherhood had chosen a *new* vessel for its rebirth. For the past four centuries, the secret society has been at the forefront of every major medical advance in the world…"

I swallowed painfully. *Oh boy.*

"In today's world, the descendants of the surviving Blackheart Circle exist as the board of directors of Clover Pharmaceutical. We have endured for a full millennium. When we were poised for power and the magic failed us, we turned to medicine—biding our time in a world that never saw us lurking in its shadows. Our efforts birthed Earth's largest international provider of medicine, a great charitable healthcare foundation, and an incredibly productive medical research division. All of this is in preparation for the fated day when magic finally returns to our world—through the twelve rifts that sent it away in the first place."

"Rifts?"

"Yes. Twelve rifts across the world sucked away our magic a thousand years ago—lying dormant for all these years. We know their general locations—two in Europe, one in Africa, four in the Americas, three in Asia, one in the Middle East, and one in Australia. We have been funneling countless funds into powering experimental technology to detect magical activity, although none of it could be tested—at least not until a year ago, when a traveler first passed between the worlds and activated this rift. Not even a month later, that traveler returned—and for a year, nothing."

Clara's disappearance...

"But then, something *interesting* happened at that rift, didn't it?" Vera smirked sharply. "As we understand it, the traveler made a quick passage through and back—but *this* time, they were not alone... and with a *vampire* on this world, our scanners did the work of *decades* in just three short days. It seems we were just minutes too late to capture it."

"So the lake..."

"That lake is the rift of Western Europe, one of the twelve. The rest of the Clover board doesn't believe the texts—they consider talk of Rifts to be the wishful ramblings of our predecessors. I'm not like the others, Peter. I've always believed—yet I never thought I'd live to see the day..."

I coughed; the taste of copper lingered in my throat. "So, you get your hands on a vampire—or, I don't know, a magical creature of *some* kind. What then? You prove that you were right? You try to get more? Or do you hold the world hostage?"

"Hostage? What do you mean?"

"You threaten to spread vampirism?"

Vera chuckled. "Clever! Peter, you should have been one of us. No one on my team has suggested that one. Maybe I should offer you a job..."

"What do you need from magical monsters?"

"Not *monsters*, plural. I only need one."

"For… what?"

Vera Partridge smiled evilly. "That depends. Are we friends, Peter Tatham? *Really* friends? I advise you to think very carefully before you answer…"

I tried to laugh again. "What happens if I say 'no'?"

"Do you like living?"

"It beats the alternative."

"Then don't answer 'no.'"

"Ah," I sighed painfully. "We're friends."

Vera narrowed her eyes, summing me up.

"Just don't have them hit me again. I've gotta be honest, that makes it hard for me to…" I coughed. "To be friends."

"You weren't *cooperating.*"

"I was trying to. You weren't listening."

"You helped me lose my prey. I *know* that there was a vampire headed for that lake, along with a traveler…"

I thought of that bizarre, growling vampire.

And I thought of my closest friend, Clara.

"She was my friend," I told her.

"The vampire was your friend?" Vera asked, a look of curiosity replacing her tight-lipped grin.

"The traveler, as you call her," I coughed painfully. "The *traveler* is my friend."

She smiled curiously. "And you helped them escape this world? You admit it, then?"

"Yes," I swallowed blood. *Please don't ever come back here, Clara. I can't betray you, but they'll kill me—and that vampire of yours promised to keep you **safe** this time…*

Vera Partridge watched me, taking a deep breath. For a moment, I thought she had made her decision—the one that would leave me alone and bleeding in the darkness of this facility.

"So, why are you telling me all of this then? Surely it isn't just because I asked…"

"Oh, I'm not simply telling *you*. I'm telling another; one who has long deserved an explanation. *You* are just a convenient excuse to do so, particularly if you prove to be *useful* in the future…"

Vera turned meaningfully to the security camera in the corner. I trailed her gaze until she glanced back with renewed energy.

"The brotherhood has existed by surviving through the centuries in multiple forms—each time failing, each time rising. *Clover* has existed since the nineteenth century, but we chose this form for a *practical* reason. Tell me, Peter, have you ever heard the term 'panacea'?"

I grunted. "Doesn't really ring a bell."

"The Greeks believed in a goddess who embodied universal remedy. They called her *Panacea*. Her name gives us the term for a theoretical cure-all. It so happens that our ancient texts are very clear on a minor detail: the blood of a magical creature is said to have *staggering* medicinal properties and applications."

In a heartbeat, I saw where this was going.

And I *really* didn't like it.

"After a thousand years of adapting and surviving, Clover Pharmaceutical has poised itself to synthesize a panacea from spellbound blood."

"So, you're going to sell it to the world?"

"We have wealth. You're thinking too small."

"Then…" My eyes widened. "Oh."

"Scarcity breeds power. Clover will have the most demanded resource on the planet—*everlasting* health. With that at our disposal, we will approach every *truly* influential family in the world—the 1% of the 1%. We will offer them eternal immunity for nothing less than eternal influence. Clover will always have a seat at the table…"

I swallowed tenderly. "You want to rule the world?"

Vera smiled triumphantly, her eyes flaring in pride. "After a thousand years, we stand ready to *finally* fulfill the dreams of our ancestors, the Blackheart Circle. With our guiding hand, we can finally put an end to war and poverty, misery and sickness, death and destruction. Imagine what humanity could accomplish if it was unshackled from its *fragile* mortality. Think of what we could do if we only had the gift of *time.* But we need to forge a place of influence to keep things… on track."

There's no way she didn't see the horror in my eyes.

"Don't you see, Peter? We don't want to rule this world. We want to *save* it…"

CHAPTER 14
ELLIOTT

The lords looked aghast as I ended the story. In the light cast from the stained windows, I could tell that the afternoon was getting on without us.

I tried my best to keep my eyes off the conspicuously empty seat beside me. *It would have been so much easier to have this fated conversation with you by my side. You had to go and choose **this moment** to be difficult...*

"I, for one, refuse to believe it," Valentine glowered. "Are we to believe in a world bent on destruction beneath a fiercely burning sun? Young lord, you try to make fools of us all."

"I thought you might say that..."

I rose from my seat, slowly tugging the gloves from my wounded hands before holding up my scarred and burned palms. Hushed fear mounted across the table as the vampire lords—even Valentine Vasiliev—recoiled in collective horror.

Chanda Song squeaked in fear. "What... *happened?*"

"The sunlight nearly destroyed me," I responded firmly. "I

opened a door and was bathed in it. I held up my hands to protect my face, and my body was overwhelmed with an unnatural and gripping agony. My lords, I couldn't move... I couldn't *breathe*... I burned *everywhere*..."

The horrors of that moment forever seared into my mind. The flashback threatened to fully overcome me; I tried to relax and keep still.

Don't let them see you in that kind of fear.

"Why haven't they healed?" Svetlana asked.

"I have no answer to your question. If the most basic dangers of the human world overwhelm and subjugate the healing powers of a *vampire lord,* then think what they might do to a vampire of *common* blood."

The harrowing memories slowly receded as I once again reached for the gloves, slipping them carefully over my scarred hands. "I received these burns on the first morning I was on her world. I believe my palms absorbed the most sunlight..."

Ooktuk Krum scratched at his bald, smoothed head. "You spoke of your grievous injuries, and yet, only your palms remain burned?"

I paused. I'd meant to keep them *away* from that.

"Yes, Lord Elliott," Valentine leaned forward. "If you were *bathed* in sunlight, tell us how you were able to return so *unscathed*..."

"Blood," I replied coolly, choosing the remain honest in this discussion.

Eyes-Like-Fire tilted her head. "What *kind* of blood? You've described such different creatures on her world. Surely, it was a beast of great power."

Svetlana tapped against her temple in thought; her eyes flashed as she glanced my way. "Human?"

The others turned to me with collective interest.

"Yes," I revealed hesitantly. "Human blood."

Chanda Song swallowed. "Was it…? *Clara's?*"

I nodded.

"You have tasted the blood of the human," Svetlana observed dispassionately. "And you did not see fit to tell us this without being questioned—why *is* that?"

"I feared your reaction," I replied. "*All* of your reactions. I did not take Clara's blood of my own free will. She forced it upon me to save my life."

"You may recall that you promised to tell us *everything,*" Valentine noted darkly. "If you are *unwilling* to cooperate with that, we can dismiss you from the table."

"There is no reason to threaten me," I sighed.

"We are not threatening you."

I glanced at the empty seat next to mine.

"My lords, I have offered you everything that I know. With this revelation, we have no secrets between us. I assure you, the human world is a terrifyingly dangerous place, and we should Unless there is something I've overlooked, or you feel I have not explained adequately…" I let my words trail off for a moment.

The vampire lords sat in silence, exchanging looks. I felt very tired then, partly from the forgotten dreams that kept me half-dazed and terrified, but also from my newfound complete lack of fight concerning the human in my castle. *There is nothing more I can do now, Clara. I have given this everything that I have, even without you…*

I snapped out of my thoughts as Mattias Blackburn turned

to me with a stern glare. "Lord Craven, could you give us the room?"

I raised an eyebrow. "Of course..."

"Thank you for your understanding."

The lords sat together and waited expectantly until I rose from my seat. *They're voting* **already?** *Has the moment that will define her fate finally come?* My hands were tied; there was nothing more for me to do but wait for them to declare her destiny.

"I will be outside," I stated as I rose from the table.

I closed the door behind me; my mind was a clutter of whispering thoughts and scrambling fears. Even with her latest little rebellion, I felt that Clara Blackwell did not deserve to disappear into The Drenchlands for a few rounds of Svetlana's *testing,* or into the melancholic depths of Valentine's idea of *care* within The Wastes...

To my complete lack of surprise, Nikki Craven stealthily swept down to the floor beside me, leaving a small cloud of dust hit the air in her wake.

"You came after all," I replied dryly.

"Of course. I wasn't going to miss the party."

I crossed my arms, glancing up at the corner of the hallway. "How did you get inside?"

Briefly brushing herself off, Nikki rose to her boots and wiped away several strands of platinum golden hair from her eyes. "Mother always held her big meetings here. When I was younger, I explored the secrets of the castle... including the chrysm service cooridors that run between the walls. If you know the way, it isn't hard to get around—for me at least." She appraised me with an amused look. "For someone of *your* build and height, it would be a bit more difficult..."

"You're climbing around *inside* the walls?"

She smiled mischievously. "Don't act surprised."

"How could I possibly," I instinctively rolled my eyes.

Nikki peered curiously. "What was *that?*"

"What was *what?*"

"The eye thing you just did there."

"Oh. This?" I rolled my eyes again.

"Yeah, that. What's that?"

"Rolling my eyes?"

"What does it mean?"

"Clara says it conveys mild to rampant annoyance—if it's among loved ones, generally in a *fond* way, like a feigned sigh of disbelief."

Her eyes lit up with a teasing smile. "Oh, my brother dearest, has the human world *already* started rubbing off on you?"

"Knock it off," I snorted.

She rolled her eyes.

"Yes, like that."

"Oh good! Seems I've gotten it down already. When I grow up, can I be a real human too, Elliott? Like you?"

I sighed. "How much of that did you hear, then?"

"Of what?"

"Don't be daft." I glanced at the sealed door. "How much did you hear?"

She smiled wickedly. "*All* of it."

"And you saw fit to leave me alone in there?"

"We have different roles to play, you and I..." Nikki slipped an arm around me and led me to a nearby corner of the room, into the shadows. "You work in the light, openly agreeing to their whims for the sake of diplomacy. That is your great strength..."

She took a step backward from me. "But mine, dear brother, is to lurk in the darkness. Watching... *waiting*... and above all, my Elliot, forever *learning*..."

The door behind me clattered, and then opened.

I turned to it in surprise, but I already heard a slight scrape of boots against stone and palms scraping walls; sure enough, Nikki Craven had already vanished from sight—quietly returning to whatever hole she'd crawled from...

Chanda Song's melodic voice wafted into my ears. "Lord Craven, if you could accompany me inside..."

Watching...

Waiting...

*And above all, my Elliott, forever **learning**...*

"Lord Craven?" She asked after me, curiously.

I shook Nikki's words from my head as I turned her way. "Forgive me, Lord Song. I have... a *lot* on my mind."

Chanda smiled sympathetically. "Of course, Elliott. I cannot fathom the burdens you have to bear. But it will all be over soon." Linking her arm in mine, the beautiful vampire lord led me back inside.

I hope so.

ॐ

"LORD CRAVEN," MATTIAS SPOKE AS CHANDA SONG AND I TOOK our seats again. "I hope that you appreciate the *delicate* situation the Council of the Eight Holds finds itself in..."

"I do not envy it," I replied thinly.

"No," he leaned back, surmising me with a distantly searching look. "I imagine not."

The others all trained their eyes on me.

This is it, I thought. *This is the moment—*

"Do you, Lord Craven, concede to obey the decisions made by this council? Do you swear fealty to the Council of the Eight Holds in this choice, to uphold it—without restraint, without second considerations, even *if* it isn't to your obvious benefit?"

The others leaned forward in unison. Everything in me wanted to fight them on this. Every last ounce of me demanded to resist them, down to the bone—

"I will uphold your decision," I replied firmly.

The vampire lords glanced among themselves—the expressions on their faces betrayed surprise. *Not terribly hard to imagine* **why**. *From their perspectives, I have not been exactly cooperative thus far...*

"Say that again," Mattias commanded assertively.

I set my jaw defensively. Especially after the burst of fury from Clara earlier, the strength had been utterly ripped out of me. *I have no more power left to fight this...*

"I will abide by this council and its choice."

In my blank, drifting gaze, I spotted smirks lighting up on their faces. *Yes. Revel in it. Take your victory...*

Lord Mattias Blackburn rose from his seat, directly across the table, to powerfully stare me down. "We lords have decided thusly, united at this table: Clara Blackwell will not stay in this castle."

It wasn't a surprise, but it still wounded. All I could do was keep my jaw set and my eyes disinterested—*that way, they'll never see my betrayal coming...*

"She will leave for *six* days."

That pricked my ears. "Sorry... what?"

"We had intended to interview Clara Blackwell here in this

meeting, but she declined the invitation. We are, however, not without mercy—and her reaction gives us a new, far more *compelling* possibility... one that offers a much more interesting way to solve our problems."

I did not like where this was going.

Mattias continued: "Clara will spend one day in the castle of each of our holds, where we will question her in private. On the seventh day, she shall then return to this castle—where the Council of the Eight Holds will convene and determine her ultimate fate."

"You...?" The words failed me.

Valentine cut in with a dangerous smirk. "Lord Craven, you've had her all to yourself, and I promise you that she will be returned. For now, you need to learn to *share*. You will remain here."

"You're taking her for six interrogations, followed by a trial?"

"If you choose to think of it that way, yes," the lord of The Drenchlands offered. "We have had so *little* time within the company of your fascinating human. A trial sounds barbaric —but it is true that the impressions Clara leaves us with will factor heavily into what we decide to do with her."

"There is something that you should know." The words had escaped my lips before I knew that I'd said them... but there was no going back now. "Clara's world lacks magic, yes, but she clearly possesses unique power among humans. She wishes to nurture her magical talents."

The others considered that for a moment.

Ooktum Krum stroked at his face, lost in thought. "A human witch... I wonder if she could be *powerful*."

"I do too," Valentine noted. "I will allow this."

That surprised me. "You will?"

"Of course I will. Don't be taken aback, Lord Craven. If the human is to stay in our world, then the least she could do is find a way to be *useful*. She has already proven her magical affinity. We are dealing with global calamity, and Clara may play a role in stoping it." The lord narrowed her eyes my way. "Better a useful ally in these coming times... so long as the human is willing to *share* her power, and not be *exclusive* to Stonehold..."

I wasn't sure what to make of that—but I also wasn't in a position to make demands of the council, considering the fact that they hadn't destroyed my hold and taken what they wanted by force.

"You have all been just and sympathetic," I replied calmly as I carefully chose my words. "You offer me a great deal of trust. I have no desires to *betray* that trust... but... how can I *know* that the girl will be returned?"

"We all have a vested interest in her safety," Mattias replied. Any lord who threatens her safety will be an enemy to us all. We must understand Clara's arrival and any connection she has to the disasters this world is so bravely facing. We shall honor the terms of this agreement, and you have our word that she will be passed between holds without harm."

"I will not interfere," I replied quietly.

"See that you do not, young lord," Valentine replied icily. "The actions of your immediate predecessor have kept you alive. Prove Lorelei Craven wrong, and we will not hesitate to destroy you."

With those words, I relinquished control of Clara's destiny. No longer could I shield her from the vampire lords.

For her defiance, Clara would be wrenched away from the safety of my castle... and from my own personal protection.

It left us in very dangerous territory. Nothing was certain anymore.

I've done everything that I can, my love. It's all up to you, now...

CHAPTER 15
NIKKI

Once the vampire lords had vacated the room, I shifted stone back into place and carefully crept away from the meeting chamber.

Clawing my way through ancient, forgotten crawl spaces and millennia-old dust, I replied on the keenness of my night-eyes. I rapidly worked my way over ceilings and under floors, digging back toward my entry point—an innocent crack in the corner of a storage room.

Pausing, I listened very carefully for any passersby. When none were to be found, I slipped out the forgotten little recess.

How many could you have killed?

"None," I snarled under my breath.

*Surely at least **one**...*

"I suppose I should be *happy* you left me alone this long," my impatient voice simmered. "It isn't like you to give me so much free reign."

The whisper in my head didn't respond; I ignored it and lifted my casual walk to a run.

It didn't take me long to find Clara Blackwell. Once I broke out of the servant's hallways and raced along the castle walls, I quickly discovered her with her beloved Knightly Trio in one of the lesser studies—reading from some of the collected fictional literature in the castle.

"Nikki?" She dropped the book to an end table and jumped up to hug me. "I've barely seen you since returning!"

Taken aback, I relaxed into the hug.

"You have such a curious way of greeting those who have threatened to *eat* you," I smirked as I threaded my arms around her. "What is this emotion? Is it *jealousy?* Jealousy, that I haven't tasted your blood, unlike that *brother* of mine..."

Clara relinquished her grip. Curiously, a displeased look crossed her face. "He told you about that?"

"Not *directly,* per se," I answered with a shrug.

"Overheard him, then?" She looked even angrier.

Her irritation amused me, especially given the kind of position she'd forced herself into—and *oh, how I relish telling you what you've done...*

"Yes," I replied coyly.

"Fine. Who was he telling? Lorelei?"

The knife twisted in my heart. Instead of plunging a blade into her chest for daring to speak so *flippantly* of our deceased mother, I took a deep breath. *That's right,* I told myself. *Clara doesn't know—and I won't be the one to do it. She's **his** pet... **Elliott** can be the one to break that news...*

"No," I answered coolly. "The vampire lords."

The Knightly Trio started paying attention.

"He was talking to them?" She asked. "Do I need to get ready?"

*Oh, this is going to be **fun**...*

"Nikki... what are you smiling like that?"

"No," Viktor gasped. "Don't *tell* us that it's—"

"You're a little late," I replied, barely containing my wicked satisfaction. "It seems they pulled Elliott aside and demanded the convening, with or without you.

Clara's irritation turned *deliciously* self-righteous.

"Why didn't he come get me? I thought that he needed me to be there."

"He *did* need you to be there," I agreed.

"Then why didn't he—?"

"He *tried*," I reminded her. "*You* didn't come."

"But... I thought that it was..."

"Little human, allow me to treat you to a lesson I learned very quickly in my time on the mainland," I slid an arm around her. "Pick your battles *delicately*..."

She shook her head. "There's no way that I—"

"*You* did this," I poked the side of her head firmly. "I watched him try to retrieve you. They wouldn't let him leave the presence of the council. It was a test of sorts... to see just how readily you'd come to your own judgment. You had a seat at the table, but you turned it down. It seems that your pride has denied you a voice, for the vampire lords made a decision without you—and without *him.* He fought on a pillar of sand in your absence."

I released her and drew away, trying to shove down my hunger for malice to be sympathetic. "If you had *been there,* they would have factored your wishes into their ultimate decision—but it's just too late. The vampire lords have made their choice. Worse still, they've forced Elliott to *agree* to it, on penalty of death if he refused."

"Oh god," I gasped. "They *wouldn't.*"

"Don't think for a moment that you understand the hearts of the vampire lords," I told her. "We are all living on borrowed time. If they felt that you were stacking the deck against them, they would not hesitate to act."

I watched Clara drop into a chair and cover her face in her hands. Her friends gathered around her; the one named Wilhelm placed a gloved palm on her upper back to try and comfort her. There was a conspicuous lack of *I told you so* that I didn't care for, but to each their own...

She glanced up at me, holding back tears.

"Nikki... what happens now?"

Before I opened my mouth to answer, I could hear the sounds of frantic footsteps. Right on schedule, my brother burst into the room.

"Clara..."

"I've updated her on everything she missed," I informed him. "But not on what comes next. Seems like that's a touchy subject, so I'll let you do the honours."

The human glanced between us. "Is it that bad?"

Elliott composed himself. "It's bad."

The two sides of my head battled as I leaned against a bookcase, folding my arms. Half of my mind reveled in the knowledge that Clara did this to herself—that all her time off our world, while my brother suffered, led up to this coming punishment. But the other half reached out for her, sympathizing in her plight—and it understood that separating them again hurt Elliott as well.

The Knightly Trio drifted over to my side, eager to give the two of them some room. They weren't exactly pleased to be left alone near me, but I didn't mind that.

I smirked at the funny one. "How's it going?"

Wilhelm looked at me curiously. "Me?"

"Sure."

"Oh. Uh, not bad."

"No? How's the head holding up?"

"The head?"

"Yeah, the last time I really saw you…"

His brow furrowed. "We saw each other yesterday. You had Kinsey find us on the mainland, remember? We talked in your throne room for a bit? The vampire lords showed up, and we were backing you up? Does… *any* of that ring a bell there?"

"*Before* that, I meant."

"What, with the traitor? Sabine?"

"Yes, that part. If I recall correctly, you took quite a hit. Just wanted to see if you'd suffered any long-term damage."

Wilhelm's eyes narrowed. "*You* did that."

"Hence my undying *concern*," I smirked coyly.

"Well, I think I've gotten worse at long division, but otherwise I'm alright," he shrugged. "This might be a treat for you—I kept your little note."

"You did?" My eyes widened with glee.

He dug around in his armor and produced a folded bit of paper. "Your little *apology* note for thwacking us in the stairwell. I was more than a little upset about that… but then you drew that little picture of the duck on it, and I thought, 'How bad could she *really* be, if she took the time to draw a duck?'"

"Did you really?" I grinned flirtatiously.

"Of course not," he looked me in the eyes. "You're a bloody *lunatic*!"

I slipped a finger under his chin and smirked evilly. "You are *already* smarter than most of the vampires I've ever met."

My eyes narrowed cruelly. "There might just come a day when you'll have to put me down. Do you really think that you could?"

He swallowed uncomfortably.

"Assume I'm asleep," I drifted my face closer to his, relishing in his discomfort. "Sick. Powerless. Imagine I am incapable of defending myself—but oh so *deserving* of decapitation." I bit my lip and repeated the question. "Do you think you could do it?"

Wilhelm's poor little heart was beating so hard.

"No," he answered.

I relinquished my finger from beneath his chin in a sharp little scratch, making him wince with the freshly drawn blood. "Perhaps you are not so smart after all."

I fold my arms as he wiped a thumb at the new cut. "It isn't wise to keep mementos from the deranged, little bat. They might begin to think you *like* them. Consider that mark as a *better* keepsake—more fitting, perhaps."

The other two watched us silently.

"Did *you* keep my notes?"

"Hell no," Asarra snorted.

"Do you think *you* could kill me, if you *had* to?"

The young guard smiled. "I would relish the opportunity."

Ooh, I thought evilly. *Now **her**, I like...*

"I even believe you," I smirked. "*Almost.*"

Before she could respond, Elliott stepped from Clara's side and marched up to me.

"What's that look in your eye?" I asked curiously.

"We don't have much time," he informed me. "Get everyone together in the grand hall. Before they take Clara, I need to hold a meeting with whatever subjects are available."

I looked between the two of them.

"I see what you're doing."

"Again, we don't have much time…"

I smirked. "Don't worry. Be ready in half an hour… I'll find enough to fill the room."

Viktor scratched at the back of his neck. "Wait—I'm lost here. What's going on?"

I merely smiled as I darted from the room.

Elliott, you sly dog! I suppose now's as good a time as any…

CHAPTER 16
CLARA

I watched Nikki and the Knightly Trio drift across to the side of the study as Elliott sat down beside me.

"She told me my fate was decided," I told him sadly.

Elliott gazed into space. "That's *sort of* accurate. The vampire lords are taking you tomorrow morning."

With one glance at the defeated look on his face, all of my self-righteous anger fizzled away. My frustrations with him suddenly seemed so very... *naïve.*

"Are they... honestly going to take me away?"

"Yes," he sighed wearily. "I couldn't stop them."

"Then let's run away," I nodded hopefully. "You and me. Let's just go somewhere that they can't find us."

"There is no such place," he noted calmly.

"We could go back to my world, right?"

"The light on your world nearly killed me. It's mid-day, and even if you could control our passage between worlds, can you promise me a dark space for our arrival?"

"Surely *you* have something up your sleeve."

"I did..." He looked my way. "But when you wouldn't come, it restrained me. Alone against the lords, there was very little I could do."

"What about Nikki? Why didn't *she* help?"

"Nothing good that would have come of her presence in that chamber. Even *she* knows that. The best thing she could do was hide and learn. She's particularly good at it. Even *I* didn't realize she was nearby until she *wanted* me to know..."

I looked away in grief. "I'm sorry."

"Yeah," Elliott nodded distantly. "I'm sorry too... for *everything.*"

My hand found his; he closed his grip around it.

"So, what are they going to do with me?"

Elliott sighed. "You'll spend the next six days in the other holds—all except the Falvian Badlands. You will be speaking directly with the vampire lords on a one-by-one basis. They'll pull back the veils over their lives, giving you a level of accessibility most vampires can only *dream* of."

"That doesn't sound so bad," I noted hopefully. "A world tour of castles..."

"They will be judging your every move: learning who you are, and what you could *be*. Their intentions appear to be kinder than I imagined, but I cannot deduce their ulterior plans. When they have finished, you will be returned to me. We will reconvene the Council of the Eight Holds. That's when the vampire lords will vote to decide what becomes of you."

"They couldn't reach a decision," I realized.

"They decided *not* to. Not yet."

"Why?"

"They believe you may have a connection with the perils facing our world. Your presence may be an opportunity to repair our broken world..."

"An opportunity..." I whispered.

"You have to grasp what you're giving up in response."

"And what's that?"

"Stability and safety," he answered bluntly. "Clara, you cannot treat this like a fun trip abroad. These are the most powerful and cunning vampires in the whole world—*each* of them with a vested interest in claiming you for themselves. They will not be your friends. They are *expert* manipulators, and their loyalty never extends far from their own holds."

My first instinct was to think he was exaggerating. He was wrong about them before.

Then again—that kind of thinking is what got you two into this mess to begin with, isn't it? If you'd just set aside your pride and realized that he's **always** *been on your side, maybe you wouldn't be dragged away from him like this...*

"I understand," I sighed. "What do I need to do?"

"For now?" Elliott chuckled despairingly. "The lords have given us one night before they demand you, so my suggestion would be..." He hesitated for a moment, but his warm glance met my eyes again. "...To *enjoy* it. But first, there is something that I must do."

"Oh? What is that?" I asked curiously.

Elliott merely smiled. "Wait here."

He rose and wandered over to the others. I watched as he spoke to Nikki for a moment; she briefly turned to me, and a moment later she was leaping straight out the window.

"What was all that about?" I asked as he returned.

"You'll see very shortly…"

⚜

I'D NEVER SEEN THIS MANY VAMPIRES FILLING THE EXPANSIVE throne room. Forming a crowded throng on either side, they left open a central aisle for the procession to use. The Knightly Trio and I took a place near the front, and we watched Nikki Craven and her royal guards—Kinsey among them—march up to the throne.

Elliott's sister looked unusually downcast.

I wonder if everything's okay…

Nikki paused just shy of the throne, turning back to address the rest of us. "Subjects of the castle, thank you for setting aside time from your rather *busy* little lives to join me here. It is a matter of importance to…"

She hesitated, looking away.

I'd known Nikki to be unhinged on her better days, but this wasn't like her. *Something* was eating her up on the inside. I quickly made up my mind to ask her about it as soon as this was over—at least, *whatever* it was that she had in mind for drawing all of these people together.

A sly smirk slipped across her expression as she glanced over the crowd. "You know, we have so *many* of these little meetings lately, haven't we? The world used to move so much slower…"

Her smile faded; Nikki stared off into space as her voice trailed off. I wondered for a moment if she'd even forgotten any of us were here with her.

She finally continued, as if the moment of silence had never happened. "In the past few years, our beloved Stonehold has changed in great, sweeping strides—and so too has the rest of the world. Dangerous things are on the horizon. There's just no going back now…"

Nikki Craven folded her arms introspectively as she stared at the crowd, biting her lip. *I've never seen her so composed,* I realized. She shook her head, lost deep in her own thoughts. "But I didn't call all of you here to discuss any of that. In fact, it wasn't really me who called you at all. There is another who wants to speak to you."

Inquisitive murmurs rolled across the crowd.

Nikki flicked her wrist. "Brother?"

The murmurs only rose in volume as Elliott Craven moved out from the shadows. He was at her side within an instant, cold and brooding as ever.

With a lazy glance at the throne, he decided to stay with her instead. It didn't escape my notice that both Cravens had rejected it in front of the crowd, choosing instead to speak directly among the people. Nor did I miss how he spoke in her ear briefly; when she shook her head, they briefly exchanged a meaningful look.

What is going on?

Elliott stepped forward, gazing far along the crowd. "As you have no doubt heard—I have returned to Stonehold Castle. There are those among you who have already seen me, or noticed the return of the human girl…"

His eye caught mine, and I shrank in shame.

"…But it's probably time that I made a formal announcement, so here it is," he replied confidently and firmly. "I have crossed between worlds—and I brought Clara back from the human realm."

The nearest vampires glanced at me with a mixture of curious interest and confused fear. The Knightly Trio instinctively drew a little closer around me.

"There is more."

The crowd slowly quieted down.

"It has come to my attention that the way that I've been ruling Stonehold for the past year has been... *unpopular*," Elliott narrowed his eyes accusingly. "There are reasons for my choices, all of which I have made carefully and with the hold's prosperity in mind. I do not feel, as your sworn ruler and protector, that it is necessary for me to explain myself... or *any* of my actions..."

IIe began walking down the aisle within the crowd; the dark, withering glare of the vampire lord made most of his subjects shrink in fear. *No, Elliott,* I wept within my mind.

"But..." he stopped. "I will."

I thought maybe I'd misheard him at first. Wilhelm and I shared a curious look.

Elliott sighed. The scene looked iconic to me—with an impossible throng of vampires on either side, silently watching, there stood the young vampire lord with his shoulders bowed and a powerful expression on his face. If he had reached out both arms, so close they were, he would have brushed both his wrists against the faces of vampires. Elliott had the attention of most of his castle; I didn't envy the pressure he must have felt beneath all those eyes, silently judging him...

"In Clara's absence, I lost my way," he told them. "I can

admit that. The last year has… *challenged* me. It was *my* decision for her to leave. In my spiraling remorse after her departure, I became something less than I am."

He lifted his eyes; for a fleeting moment, they made contact with mine. "For that, I hope you'll forgive me."

The vampires shared quiet glances around him. In their murmurs, I could see their expressions changing—*for the better, I hope.*

"You all know that I have prepared myself for the anger of the vampire lords—and they are here on the Isle of Obsidian. Our castle still stands. Blood still pumps within my veins. I was deeply mistaken in their intentions—and thanks to your former lord, Lorelei Craven…"

His voice briefly cracked.

"…Their minds were changed. We stand at the cusp of a new era of peace—a fragile and careful peace, but a peace nevertheless. We will be a world united again!"

The crowd cheered. A number of meaningful looks came my way, but I was paying attention to Elliott. His expression didn't change—if anything, he looked *sadder*. When he glanced over, his eyes searched for his sister… and she shared the same blank, unmoved look.

It was like they barely cared how popular that was.

As the crowd finally settled down, Elliott continued to walk between his people. "It is one thing for me to say that things will change—it is quite another to see it for yourself. That is why I am instituting some changes to the way I run this castle…"

He held up his thumb. "I will make myself much more accessible to *you,* the subjects of this castle, to answer your concerns and fears. Every Thursday night at sundown, you will find me in front of Craven Keep for a questioning period. You are free to ask anything of me, or to question the choices I have made. I expect to be asked many questions about the things I experienced in the human world, and I will answer your questions without restraint."

The crowd was visibly moved. I could see how they looked upon their ruler with a softer gaze; I wondered if he knew what he was doing, opening himself up to all of them like this. Still holding up his thumb, he added his index finger.

"I promise that I will roll back some of my *harder* and less popular decrees from this past year. No matter my intentions to protect us, I understand that I went too far. If the vampire lords stay true in their cooperation, then my hard choices no longer present the *best* option for this hold's long term survival."

He added another finger.

"Three—the succession. We have spoken, and there has been a final, binding decision... but I'll let her tell it however she chooses."

Nikki walked down the steps and stood at his side, looking among the subjects. "I never wanted to rule—and I think I've been *really clear* on that one. None of you wanted me in that fancy chair to begin with." Her eyes lit up with a wicked smile. "Not that I blame you, really. Putting me there was an *incredibly* stupid decision. I will relinquish the throne to my brother. He will rule Stonehold as the *single* vampire lord. In exchange, I retain my claim to the Craven name, as granted by the heads of the castle. For now, I will serve close to the throne as..."

She glanced at him. "I can't say it."

"Do you want me to do it for you?"

"Yeah. Fine."

Nikki folded her arms and looked away, crossly.

"Nikki Craven was my vassal—and although the complexities of my departure made this ambiguous, she will return to my service," Elliott declared. "My sister shall *remain* my vassal, as a personal guardian and a trusted advisor. Along with Kinsey, she will help me rule this hold..."

He held up another finger.

"...Which brings me to my last change to the castle. As the vampire lord, I will remain the sole master of this hold... but I will not rule alone. In these uncertain, dangerous times, I must ensure that the darkness of this past year never overcomes me..."

All eyes carefully watched him. As much as they hung on his every last word, I probably could've heard a *cough* from halfway down the hall.

"...I *will* lean more heavily on my vassals and my subjects for their wisdom and guidance."

He found Kinsey in the crowd and locked eyes with her. "...And so, I promise to you all that I will take their opinions into far greater consideration. If I am to truly be a ruler worthy of your support, then I must learn to trust others in the decision-making process. No matter what comes... *we are all in this together.*"

This time, when the assembled vampires cheered, they did it for *him.* Clearly taken by no small surprise, Elliott Craven gazed around his subjects with a confused but humbled expression.

Nikki whispered something into his ear; he smiled.

A stern voice beside me drew my attention. "What do you

know?" Viktor chuckled, shaking his head. "Maybe you got through to him after all…"

I held back a small smile.

That's the Elliott I know and love.

If only I'd gotten a little longer with him before the vampire lords returned…

CHAPTER 17
CLARA

The bittersweet afternoon stung at my heartstrings.
Elliott and I stood beside together before the might of the chrysm portal. The vampire lords approached me one by one, greeting me and wishing to see me soon. All I could afford these powerful creatures was a restrained smile and a polite nod. Given the stakes held tenuously in the balance, the very last thing that I wanted to do was displease them.

They represented our greatest threat, and they had come for us in the end. It might not have quite as overt an attack as Elliot suspected, but they were still here—and ready to separate us.

Each one passed by the gatekeeper.

Each was sent back to their castle...

All but one.

Nikki smirked. "Of course it would Ooktuk Krum. Looks like we're getting you started with the *weird* one, aren't we now?"

I glanced at the lord as he walked over towards us. Built thin and pale, Ooktum Krum strode over toward us in an opened olive cloak—a cloak that revealed a lean but highly muscular build. Thick, beaded armbands of a clearly tribal nature clenched to his biceps, and the only garment on him was a pair of shorts decorated in large, foreign leaves. Completing the mysterious shaman look was the bald scalp and unnaturally dark eye sockets.

"It is time," Ooktum spoke simply. "Say goodbye."

I looked to Nikki Craven first. "Advice?"

The vampire princess folded her arms confidently. "You aren't dealing with regular vampires here, Clara. Integrate yourself if you can, but don't patronize them. They want to know more about you—so give them what they want and try not to make them angry..."

"That sounds threatening. I thought Lorelei convinced them to spare me from harm..."

Her eyes darkened. "Things have changed."

She turned her gaze away before I could ask what she meant.

"The clock's ticking, little human. Better not waste the seconds you have left..."

Hastily, I turned back to the lord of Stonehold with despairing, tearful eyes. "I'm sorry, Elliott. I'll come back, I promise."

"The time to be sorry has passed," he smiled sadly. "Steel yourself for the journey. Do you have everything you need?"

I patted the sack on my back, nodding. "I think so."

Elliott pulled me into a warm, enduring embrace. Overcome with loss, I hugged the vampire back. His lips met my forehead, and he gazed into my eyes longingly.

"Be good," he whispered. "Be smart. Be resourceful. Above all, be cautious. You travel with lords as brilliant and cunning as they are dangerous. Keep your wits about you, Clara Blackwell, and come back to me safe."

"Of course," I smiled.

I planted a farewell kiss on his lips.

"Tell Lorelei I'm sorry I missed her," I whispered in his ear. If I hung back any longer, I'd lose my composure—so I turned away and walked to Lord Krum's side.

"Are you ready?" He asked me.

"I am," I nodded.

"Good." He turned toward the chrysm gatekeeper. "Take us to World's Pillar."

I couldn't help it. I turned over my shoulder for one last look at the Craven siblings as the portal roared back to life before us. Elliott's cold, miserable look said it all. As he solemnly watched us leave, Nikki was whispering something to him.

"Come."

I turned back, reluctantly following Ooktum Krum into the chrysm portal—and left behind everything familiar and known…

৯৶৯

NEVER ONCE IN MY TIME WITH ELLIOTT HAD I EVER THOUGHT I might get to see beyond the restrictions of Stonehold.

I choked, falling to my knees.

My host dropped to a knee and comforted me. "Traveling so far by chrysm is difficult on the body. Does this feel similar to your travels between worlds?"

I shook my head, swallowing back my bile.

"Will I—" I choked again. "Will I get used to it?"

The shamanic vampire lord rose to his feet again, summoning over one of his nearby guards with the click of his fingers. As the guard scurried over—dressed just like my host, minus the open cloak—Lord Krum glanced down to me with mild sympathy.

"You will *have* to."

His guard held the butt of his wooden spear against the ground as he slowly helped me up from my knees. I clutched to him for support as the sights overwhelmed my senses.

This chrysm portal was not hidden away within the basements of some dark and looming castle. It stood out in the open air, eager to put on a show for all who would dare to approach it.

As I stood clasping to the guard, I realized that my experience in this world didn't even extend to all of Stonehold. This was the first time I'd left the Isle of Obsidian, and the Stoneholdian mainland Nikki and Elliott Craven had spoken of remained a mystery even after all this time...

Pushing forward, I took hard, staggering steps with the help of the guard. In a dozen punishing strides, I clung to the wooden railing and gazed down the side to get my bearings. The sheer plummet was massive—we were easily ten stories up from the lake below.

My eyes lifted forward to the wonders before me.

I stood atop some kind of treetop fortress, facing into the sprawling immenseness of a menacing jungle... a place unlike anything I'd ever seen. The trunks of the trees surrounding us continued upward to a canopy high above, and between them was a dark, *dangerous* blackness.

"What... where am I?"

Ooktum Krum solemnly took a position at my side. "Welcome to Selvara Karn, little Clara—the lands of the forever forests and the dark-in-the-trees... of the things that eat, and of powers too strong to be restrained."

"It looks beautiful," I observed. "And terrifying."

Lord Krum nodded. "It is both. The forest of Selvara Karn covers the entire hold. It is a powerful place where magic runs rampant..." He gave me a meaningful look. "Nature is a cruel mistress here. If it were not for all the magical protections here, the castle would be overcome with carnivorous beasts and deadly plants."

"Deadly plants? Is it... *that bad* out there?"

He nodded sternly. "You see how dark it is? The canopy grows so thick that light cannot reach the ground even in the brightest of days. Nature found *another* way to sustain itself."

"How?" I asked, realizing I didn't want to know.

"Everything within Selvara Karn *eats*."

I swallowed fearfully, turning back to the forest. It *did* seem alive—very alive—and I suddenly feared what it would mean to get lost in there...

"Come with me," Lord Krum noted.

When I turned to follow him, a stunned gasp escaped from my lips. My gaze drifted up the largest tree I had ever encountered. Far above us, the boughs stretched out and formed a powerful canopy of gigantic leaves.

"Yggdrasil," I whispered.

"What is that word?" Krum asked curiously.

"Yggdrasil—the World Tree," I explained, shaking my head to clear it. "I read about something like this. In Norse mythology, they speak of a great and powerful tree,

Yggdrasil, upon which the rest of the world is built. It is a sacred place…"

"I do not know of Yggdrasil," Krum observed, "but this tree is sacred to us. It protects us as a beacon of hope shining in a jungle of teeth and bloodshed. Come."

He clicked his fingers again, and the guard released his grip on me. I steadied myself against the railing and stumbled after the vampire lord.

⚜

THE PORTAL WAS ON A LESSER PLATFORM NEAR THE TOP OF THE settlement. As Lord Krum led me further into the castle, down below the boughs and branches, I came to realize that this wasn't anything like Elliott's fortress at all—the entire stronghold was woven naturally into it's treetop environment.

World's Pillar, as it turned out, wasn't the castle at all. It was the majestic tree—and the other trees I had admired on arrival were mere branches sprouted from its roots. Together, they served as a barrier to the outward forest.

I felt a powerful thrum as I wandered from wooden deck to deck, connected by reinforced rope bridges that hung far above the lake.

*Good thing that I'm not afraid of **heights**…*

"What happens if someone falls?" I asked curiously as we crossed the third dangerously small bridge. The ceiling of leaves cast the entire world down here in shadow, so it wasn't hard to imagine—but swirling little green fires in floating glass boxes twirled in place, scattered around the entire castle to light the way.

Leading the way in our single-file line, Lord Krum

suddenly came to a stop. By now, I'd gotten used to his blank expression and near constant commitment to an apparent vow of silence—but then, for just one second, I thought saw a smile cross his lips.

His hand was suddenly on my shoulder.

"Would you like to find out?"

"Wait—what are—?"

As effortlessly as one flicks away a bug, he flung me over the side. I wailed in terror as my limbs flew out, but it was too late—the vampire lord and his entourage watched as I plummeted down, down, down, turning to face the rapidly rising lake as I instinctively clutched at the amulet clasped round my neck, desperate for anything that might stop my fall... even if it meant casting myself back out of this world.

But I never had the chance to call upon its power.

My descent slowed unexpectedly. Halfway down from where I'd been thrown, I came to a complete stop. In mid-air, I watched in amazement as a glowing cloud of sparkling dust was flickering to life around me. It twirled in a lazy storm as I gradually began to spin and ascend.

The twinkling dust lifted me all the way back up to the bridge before carefully placing me back into place in the very spot that I'd been standing.

"What was... how did...?"

"Magic, of course," the lord responded obliquely. "I've been led to believe you have some interest in witchcraft. Surely, recognize the work of a simple spell?"

My face crumpled and I burst into laughter, putting a palm to my forehead. *Of course it was magic. What else would it be?*

The lord smiled. "I am glad that you enjoyed the fall."

"I did... and I must say, your castle is magnificent."

He nodded. "It is beautiful, isn't it? It brings me joy that you can appreciate it. Selvara Karn is no stranger to the horrific, but even in the darkest depths can one find beauty—if one stops to look for it."

"I couldn't agree more," I grinned politely.

Lord Krum's smile faded. "It's a shame that you are agreeable. It makes what comes next *very* difficult for me."

Elliott's words reverberated around in my mind, like a distant warning. *You travel with lords as brilliant and cunning as they are dangerous.*

I became aware of my own heartbeat. The world around me seemed so slow and silent now. I could've sworn that the *forest itself* held its breath.

"What comes *next*?" I nervously asked.

The lord took a step closer; Ooktuk Krum tenderly placed his rough palm to my cheek. Fearfully, I bristled at the touch. "This is not some grand adventure. You have been brought to this hold for judgment. As such, you are not our guest, but our burden."

I swallowed painfully. "I don't understand."

For a fleeting moment, Lord Krum looked mildly sympathetic. "I am afraid that you'll need to forgive me, Clara Blackwell. The secrets of the vampire lords are not meant for the eyes of strangers—and certainly not the eyes of someone so dangerous. I must see what you *really* are, human. To allow you your memory of this place would allow you to fool me."

"Oh," I realized sorrowfully. "You're going to make me forget?"

"Worse," Lord Krum replied solemnly. "I am going to make you never *remember*. Your mind will be pushed down, leaving your true self for the vampire lords to study, question, and *evaluate*. We are not going to judge you based on your cunning or your intelligence. We are here to observe what is beneath it all. Only when we understand your driving nature can we choose your fate. And to do that..." The lord ordered the rest of the guards to back away with a subtle motion. "I will need to make *you* go away... for just a *little* while."

What the lord seemed to be describing some sort of magical lobotomy, and it terrified me... but I knew from staring into his dark eyes that I had no choice in the matter. Averting my gaze briefly, I sighed—the forest all around looked so beautiful and fascinating.

It would be such a shame to forget it...

"Will I come back?" I asked him. "Will I be okay?"

"Of course you will. You will be restored when we have finished—with no memories of your time here."

This was their plot, I realized with a heavy heart. This was how they would ensure that Elliott's influence over me means nothing.

"I do not need your permission... but I *shall* ask for it. Do you submit?"

"I submit," I told him. "I submit myself to the will of the vampire lords."

Lord Krum's eyes flashed in surprise. "You do?"

"I do," I nodded sadly. "I only plead that the lords let me remember *some* of this. Please, I beg you, just leave me that. This world is so beautiful—I can't bear to forget it..."

Ooktuk Krum sighed so heavily that his shoulders rose and lowered. His pensive gaze darted away, locked in deep and considerable thought.

"Whatever you decide," I noted, "I accept."

The air was so silent. Nothing else dared to move.

He did not answer. Instead, he placed a hand on my forehead, splaying the fingers. The other one reached down into his cloak, digging around in a hidden pouch. I held his stern gaze, unwilling to break it for a second—even after he withdrew something small and malleable between his fingers, like a piece of clay.

"It cannot be done. No—it *will* not be done."

I swallowed sadly. "I understand, Lord Krum."

The vampire lord held me within his commanding gaze. "Clara Blackwell, for your judgment, your time with the vampire lords will continue without your awareness. As the rulers of this world, we will study and observe you, learning your character, your spirit, and what you *truly* are."

I tried to hold a strong, defiant expression.

"I'll show you all," I told him. "I'll win you over."

He smiled, almost fondly, as he pressed something into my hair and whispered a few words. His smile faded, replaced with malcontent. The change was so rapid that my heartbeat nearly exploded inside my chest.

"And so, human, your judgment begins..."

CHAPTER 18

ELLIOTT

Throughout my afternoon meeting with Nikki Craven and high chancellor Silas, the memory of Clara leaving with Lord Krum haunted me. I'd let her slip into the jaws of darkness.

It was made worse by the fact that it might have been avoided if not for the confrontation in the castle village. Just as vivid in my mind was the sight of her furious, accusing eyes as she tore at my heartstrings.

For a moment, I let that feeling of anger linger.

I've never seen Clara like that before...

It was clear to me that people were spreading a perversion of events meant to twist what she thought of my actions. At first, I wondered how best I could properly retaliate—but the obvious conclusion was that any perceived sleight against my friends here would only weaken me in her eyes.

I'd been driven into a corner, and I hated it.

"Lord Elliott?" Silas' voice pulled me back.

"Yes?" I groaned, distracted. "What is it?"

"I'm afraid you weren't paying attention, my Lord. You *must* participate in listening to the people's needs."

"He's a bit distracted," Nikki cut in. "We both are."

"You can be *distracted* some other time," Silas chided us sternly. "I allowed you a day's solace with the vampire lords in the castle—and I really wish you'd informed me of that, instead of letting me find out the *hard* way. For now, you are the ruler of Stonehold. If Lorelei was here—"

"Lorelei Craven is dead."

The old windbag froze. "What did you just say?"

My simmering glare lowered at him. "I *said,* 'Lorelei Craven is *dead*.' She died the same night the lords came."

Silas swallowed angrily. "That is *low*, even for you."

"It's true," Nikki replied distantly.

The high chancellor glared between the two of us. "I don't believe it. Not even for a second…"

"If I can prove it, you'll leave us alone today?"

Nikki agreed. "I could use a little break myself."

◈

I PULLED BACK THE MOURNING CLOTH.

Silas held his hand to his mouth with a shock that was all too clear.

"It can't be."

"It is," I growled. "Lorelei Craven is no more."

He gazed between us, then down at the cold body of our mother on the slab. "How did…? When did…?"

I gently lowered the covering cloth back over her stern face. "We felt the passing that night—she died *peacefully*, in the gardens with Lord Blackburn."

Silas clutched at his chest. "I have to sit down."

I helped the ancient vampire out of the moratorium room and to the sitting area outside. When he was rested, he stared off into space blankly.

"You're taking this rather hard," I observed.

"Lorelei Craven was the most beloved vampire lord to ever rule Stonehold," he muttered distantly. "This is a great tragedy. We will have to announce it—"

"No," I snarled.

He looked up at me, unseeing. "What?"

"There is enough on our plates right now. Give us a week to handle the aftermath of my return. We will announce Lorelei Craven's death once I've been reunited with Clara."

"That is out of the question," Silas bitterly replied.

"We need this."

"No."

"Please," I growled. "Give Nikki and me *time* to grieve and determine a course forward. It might have slipped your mind that we have a small succession crisis to deal... thanks to your direct and foolish actions."

"I didn't realize you'd be back so soon—"

"Doesn't matter," I rebuked him. "I'm not angry with you. What's done is done, and I'm sure you had the best intentions. Still, I am now faced with difficulties on all fronts, and the thought of Clara being passed among the vampire lords has overcome my mind. I need a few days of breathing room."

I placed a warm hand on his shoulder, with a heavy sigh. "I am asking for your help, Silas—and to handle the complex needs of our subjects in the meantime. There is so much to do."

He looked up at me with annoyed eyes. I knew that he was

considering denying me this request, but the burdening chains of duty wouldn't allow it.

I will offer you a proper apology soon...

"Very well," he grumbled. "It shall be done."

I looked over my shoulder. Nikki Craven was still in the chamber—she had drawn back the mourning cloth again, staring at our mother with despairing eyes.

"Is there anything *else* I should be enlightened to?" Silas muttered, shaking his head fretfully.

A dark smile hinted along my lips.

"Actually..."

ॐ

STANDING BETWEEN MY SISTER AND I, THE BELEAGUERED HIGH chancellor vacantly stared into the dark, dank dungeon cell containing the comatose vampire lord of the Falvian Badlands. None of us had moved for several minutes—particularly not the simmering Silas.

"I don't know why I'm even surprised."

The weary tone of his voice nearly made me feel a drop of remorse for the elderly vampire—and his utterly thankless job. *Nearly.*

"I vote we kill him," Nikki noted.

Silas turned to her with an overtly disgusted look. "You left the lord of a hold rotting away in a *dungeon* cell, and you wish to kill him as he slumbers?" Stunned, he shook his head. "How could that the ramifications of his death be so insignificant to you?"

Nikki casually shrugged. "Many things are *insignificant* to me."

"Keep him alive, and properly restrained," I patted Silas on the back. "And don't let Nikki anywhere near him," I added helpfully.

"I don't believe it. *Two* vampire lords... the passing of the most beloved ruler in history... and now *this*." He glanced at me with a dumbstruck expression. "My Lord, you have been back in the castle *for two days.* Tell me, please—what *other* havocs do you intend to wreak?!"

"You know... technically, this little surprise wasn't Elliot's fault," Nikki helpfully offered. "You can thank our precious mother for our slumbering beauty."

He sputtered, glancing back at Akachi Azuzi's body. "You are both going to shuffle me to an early grave. You *do* realize that, my Lords..."

CHAPTER 19
ELLIOTT

Comfortably reclined with a boot against the fireplace, Nikki sharpened a dagger against a small whetstone in her hand. Blowing on the edge, her lazy glanced drifted my way as I continued to quietly pace the study.

"You've bought us a few days. Now what?"

I planted my hands against the mantle shelf and let my head bow. The light flickering of the dancing flames only reminded me of my burns, and that served to make me nervous—but I'd done some of my best deliberation when I was nervous.

"There is nothing I can do about the vampire lords at the moment," I replied dispassionately, working out some of the lingering details in my head. "They can hold onto their victory for now."

"Let me help. What are your goals, Elliott?"

"Protecting this hold, and keeping Clara safe."

"Good," she nodded. "What are your threats?"

"Primarily… the vampire lords."

"No," she replied sternly, her dagger slipping on the whetstone. With an annoyed sigh, she blew on the blade again and slipped it into its holster on her leather armor. "The vampire lords have made it very clear that they're open to compromising with you. They *aren't* your enemy, not unless you *make them* your enemy."

"If they aim to separate Clara and me…"

"Stop putting this ultimatum in your head, Elliott. You have a chance to keep her, but making the lords into your sworn opponents will do nothing but destroy that opportunity…"

"You're right," I realized. "I should focus on the threats closer to home."

"Closer to home…?" Nikki briefly pulled away her gaze as she considered my words—she looked back with a sly smile on her lips. "You mean the guards? You mean to punish them for getting between her and you…"

"They pitted her against me."

She bit her lip, rising up from her chair. "*Did* they?"

"Everything between us was *fine* on her world. Without their influence, we were *together* again. Our reunion has been *tarnished* by their attempts to undermine me…"

"Are you certain that's what happened?"

I glowered at my sister. "Speak carefully."

"Or what, darling brother? You'll *punish* me, too?" Nikki heartily laughed—the sound served only to mock me. "You're far too intelligent for this, Elliott. The truth is obvious. It is not their fault that you went too far, and trying to punish them a *second* time will only push Clara further away. Your only recourse here is to be better than you were—to rise above."

"Had they not been back, none of this would have happened," I muttered.

"Small reminder: you were *gone*. We had no telling *when* you might pop up again. I had a castle exploding in fear and a world ready to tear itself apart—and I needed *every* ally I could get my claws on. You could've chosen mercy in their punishments, or trained them to become more than they were, but you chose their exile."

I growled. "Don't push me right now..."

My sister smirked evilly. "I think this conversation is *long* overdue, brother." Drawing closer to my face, she glared into my eyes. "Elliott, sooner or later, you have to confront your sins..."

"Back away from me," I warned her.

"You burned bridges. You terrified your people. You flung her best friends to the distant corners of the hold, shoving them into dangerous roles, and what? What did you *think* was going to happen? You went so far, your own *vassal* turned on you in fear and self-righteousness, a vassal who nearly laid down her *life* for you a year ago. Elliott, how then, in your infinite wisdom, could you honestly expect your lack of mercy to not come back to haunt you the very *second* that she returned?"

I shoved her away.

Her hand gripped my wrist tightly. "Elliott, we both *know* that I'm right. The longer you fight the realization, the worse it will be for you in the end. You can *still* save her, but you must be *better* than this first."

I hissed angrily. "Release your grip on me."

"What will you do if I don't?" She asked curiously.

"...There's only one way to find out."

Nikki's smile widened hungrily. "Try me."

☼

THE DOORS SPLINTED OFF THE HINGES AS I HURLED BACKWARD.

Nikki descended upon me in a lunging leap. I rolled out of the way just as her boot came down *hard* against the stone flooring, catching on a rug. I whirled up to my feet and tackled her, shoving her out the open recessing walls of the hallway—this hallway had no windows, but large, open spaces between pillars.

Below? The flat earth between castle walls.

Her hand grabbed the edge of my cloak and tugged, whipping it into a choking restraint around my throat. She landed her heels against the side of the interior wall of the castle, her back to the bailey below.

I reached to unclasp the cloak, but I could barely get a grip on it before she tugged again. I lost my footing but caught a hand against a stone pillar. Several servants in the hall raced forward to help me, but it was too late.

Nikki tugged again, and I lost my grip.

As she pulled me through the empty wall, the two of us plummeted towards the castle grounds... but then again, the surging blood that coursed through our veins was the blood of the vampire lords. This simple fall was little more than an inconvenience.

We landed hard against the ground, separating in a quick bound. Panting with rage, we glared at each other in defensive positions—each one of us like a coiled viper, ready to strike at the other.

"Feel better now?" She grinned evilly.

"You threw the first punch!"

Nikki laughed. "Yes, to *encourage* you!"

"Funny way of encouraging…"

"You need to get this out of your system," my sister offered coyly. "I always think better after I've fought. It worked for Fiona, too. Maybe it's time *you* tried it."

My rage flared up in my head, and I charged at her.

Nikki and I traded blows and kicks backwards into the castle village. Tradesmen and workers darted out of sight as we passed—they scooped up their loved ones and hid away from our frenzied battle.

She blocked a kick with her raised forearm; her face spread in a taunting grin. "Come on, Elliott! I thought you were stronger than this! Are you actually gonna hit me or not?"

My fist connected with her cheek.

Nikki Craven took a few reeling steps backward as I realized in horror what I'd just done. As she finally came to a stop and steadied herself, her eyes flashed devilishly in her appraising grin. My sister wiped the side of her face with her fist, licking away a small trickle of blood.

"Nikki—I'm sorry, I didn't mean to—"

She dove toward me in a flurry of kicks. It was all I could do to parry the hardest of them; several connected against my head or in my ribs. Had I been able to focus, I might have compared the fight to our secretive training sessions further up the island.

There was no dodging her—only *withstanding* her.

My endurance against her fury had its limits. In my mounting anger, I powered through the intensity of her attacks with a head-butt; the impact dazing us both, but we stayed on our feet. Our kicks and punches became more sluggish, but we powered through the assault together until we met our impasse, collapsing in the snow in a grapple of limbs and willpower.

In my hand, I held a fistful of Nikki's hair, keeping her skull wrenched back. Meanwhile, she held a strong hand around my throat, trying to squeeze the very air out of my windpipe.

Her eye rolled down, connecting with mine.

A strained smile crossed my lips.

The two of us released our grips on each other and descended into hearty laughter. I couldn't imagine what the villagers must have thought as they slowly peaked out their heads, seeing the Craven siblings locked in a vicious fight—only for the two of us to happily concede the stalemate.

I lifted my head, realizing that a table lay crushed beneath me. Nikki rolled off of me and collapsed into the snow beside me with a sigh.

"You were right," I rose to a sitting position.

"I'm *always* right," my sister smirked.

I ignored that. "I can certainly think a little clearer..."

"I'm telling you, we're fighters. Even Mum got in on it a few days ago, remember?" Nikki sat up beside me as well, dusting sleet off of my shoulder. "You and I are all that we have now. We have to stick together. And if that means that, sometimes, I have to beat you halfway across the castle grounds—well, tough luck."

I shook my head with a smile. "Thanks."

Nikki acrobatically leapt to her feet and extended a hand. "You're welcome. So, what now, big brother? We still have a few days free."

I took it and rose to my boots.

"How do you fancy joining me for a quick trip?"

"Sure," she tilted her head. "Where are we going?"

"Bleakwood," I noted with a lingering curiosity. "I'm reminded that we still haven't caught up with Lord Blackburn. He seemed rather eager to speak with us."

Nikki folded her arms with a contemplative expression on her face. "I wonder what the old bugger wants. He *did* make it sound rather urgent…"

I nodded. "I want to dwell in the castle for a while longer, but I'll make the necessary preparations in the morning. We shall pay him a visit…"

CHAPTER 20
CLARA

I blinked in disorientation.

"Ah. I see that you've come back."

I felt my stomach turn; I clamped a hand over my mouth and clutched my gut, quickly glancing around me for something, *anything* to—

"Quick! Get her a glass! A jar! Something!"

A vase was dumped and shoved into my face. I took it and immediately emptied the contents of my stomach into it in heaving, shuddering wretches.

Oh god, I felt *miserable!*

Once the worst of it was past me, I wiped my lips with the back of my wrist and settled back into my seat. My head slumping to the side, I struggled to pull myself back together. Faintly, I was aware that someone took the vase from my hand.

"Are you quite alright?"

I felt a cool hand against my forehead. Sucking in a deep

breath, I lifted my gaze to see the vampire lord they called Svetlana Lovrić studying me with concern.

"I... what did... how did I...?

She set her jaw angrily. "You are a rather tricky one, it would appear."

I coughed heavily. "I don't understand."

"Of course you don't." Svetlana rose up and clicked her fingers. I deliriously saw that the guard holding the vase set it down and brought a glass of what looked like glowing water over toward us. With a furious look on her face, the lord held it to my lips.

"Drink."

Thirstily, I swallowed a few tentative gulps. Within seconds, I already felt the pangs of sweet relief down in my stomach. When I could bring myself to use words properly, I asked: "What *is* that?"

"It is a rejuvenating water. My scientists use it to work longer hours while performing their research, but it has health applications as well—in small doses."

I nodded. "Works like a charm..."

Svetlana rose up and pulled a chair over. As she got herself comfortable, I glanced around my environment in shock and amazement.

We seemed to be sitting in some sort of dining hall. The entire room was bathed in a dark blue, and it wasn't hard to see why—the walls to my left and right were sheets of thick glass, holding back a beautiful coral reef. A school of glowing creatures swam past; their tiny tentacles picking at particles in the water as if they were eating. The water down here was crystal clear. I could see far into the distance, where the sloping ocean floor rose up to form a large canyon. On the other side, things that were vaguely shark-like ambled past in a group.

"This is the Drenchlands," I gasped.

"You are correct," Svetlana replied firmly.

Something in her tone drew my attention. "You are angry with me," I realized. "Did I do something wrong?"

The vampire lord tented her fingers and watched in thinly veiled irritation. She snapped her gaze away for a brief moment.

"Leave us. All of you."

The guards glanced at one another. "Is that wise?"

The vampire lord narrowed her eyes. "If you question my wisdom again, you will live to regret that decision. I will be safe. Now *go*."

They reluctantly left through an automatic door.

"Wait—you have doors that open and close?"

"Of course I do. We aren't savages."

"But that's like a supermarket door—or something on a spaceship. This world seemed like it was *centuries* behind that kind of technology. How could you have this *here*, in *this* world?"

Svetlana smirked smugly. "The Drenchlands are at the forefront of all science in this world. We control inventions that would take eons for the rest of the world to naturally attain."

"Then... why not share it?"

She blinked curiously. "Why should we?"

"In my world, they say a rising tide raises all ships. Why hold science to yourself if you can have such a large impact on the world at large? Surely there's something to be gained for you out there, spreading such technology..."

Svetlana's face subtly shifted. "I already have, little human. You're undoubtedly aware of chrysm by now. It was *my* experimentation at the forefront of the chrysm revolution that swept the surface world."

"I thought it was Lorelei Craven who did that."

Svetlana's eye twitched—she sharply turned away. "Yes, Lorelei was... *instrumental.* It could not have been done without her... the vampire lord of Stonehold was highly invaluable to the project." She hesitated then, and I felt something unspoken and heavy in the air. "I'll offer you this fair warning, Clara: the wound is still very fresh. Do not speak that name again."

I didn't understand, but I nodded anyway.

"I'm sorry," I replied. "I won't, then."

"It's fine. You could not have known my connection to her. We have worked together for a very long time."

I wondered if this had anything to do with Lorelei's growing aloofness, but I thought it best not to ask. That topic was a touchy one between all the vampires I knew who were closely aware of her—it made sense to remain cautious around it, even with the vampire lords.

Or perhaps **especially** *around them...* I made myself a quick mental note to not bring her up again.

"I have a question," I asked her.

She snapped away from her thoughts. "What?"

"What's going on? I don't remember coming here..."

Svetlana snorted. A smile crossed her lips. "Well, of course you don't. You were placed beneath quite a very powerful spell. It was meant to suppress your memory and let us evaluate you at your core personality."

"A spell?"

"Tell me: what is the last thing you recall?"

"I saw... trees. Huge, sprawling trees... and there, a rope bridge... floating fires... and then..." The shudder tore right through me. "There was that *face...*"

"Ah. Was it Lord Krum?"

I nodded absentmindedly. "He... put his fingers to my forehead... he... *whispered* something..."

"Yes. *That* was the spell."

I clutched my head. I felt like I'd be sick again.

"No, no, enough of that," the vampire lord sighed. "Not everyone is going to be so amenable to your little fits of vomiting. If I were you, I'd endeavor to control your body..."

I took a few deep breaths. I opened my eyes, picking something in the room to concentrate on. In this case, it was the glass in front of me—and I realized that a half-eaten feast was between us.

"We were eating," I realized.

"We were, yes. We were having a rather interesting little conversation about ethics and philosophy. I found myself learning so much about the human approach to matters of a metaphysical nature—even with your... *limited* perspective on these things."

"He said that I wouldn't remember..."

"I'm sure he did." She turned away. Svetlana lifted a glass of what looked like blood, taking a sip from the dark, crimson drink.

"Then... how am I *aware?*"

"That's the big question, now, isn't it?" The vampire lord set the glass back down and crossed her leg, turning to me curiously. "Clara, you are *supposed* to be mentally asleep, reacting on pure instinct. Capable of holding a simple conversation, but fully unaware of your surroundings. You're meant to be operating on nothing more than your basest mind. We wanted to study your subconscious…"

She shrugged, her face borderline furious.

"And yet, here we are."

"So, I guess the spell didn't work?"

"From the looks of things… not *entirely*. I seem to recall Lord Craven mentioning your innate *resilience* to spells. I thought it was a simple misdirection, or even folly at the time, but it appears there may have been truth behind his words. You are rather uniquely capable of resisting the most powerful spells of a vampire lord—something that should be *impossible*. Nothing on this world can defy magic of this strength…"

"Is it because I'm human?"

"It could be that—or it could be the fact that you are a witch, albeit an untrained one."

"You know about that?"

"You are rather talkative, even when your awareness was a fleeting whisper. I know a very great many things about you now, Clara Blackwell, as will the others…"

"Good," I nodded to myself.

Her eyebrows rose. "You think this a *good* thing?"

"Of course I do. If I have to submit to this, then isn't it for the best that you all understand me? It's the reason why I willingly agreed in the first place."

"You agreed because you had no choice."

"I *always* have a choice," I told her. "I chose to allow myself to fall beneath this spell. I told Lord Krum to his very face that I *willingly* conceded to this."

Svetlana nodded slowly, her eyes narrowing. "This is true.

He was rather taken aback by that. To be fair, we were *all* surprised. We expected to observe you at a time of desperation and fear, but you chose a different path."

"I just want you to make the right decision."

She leaned closer, searching my gaze. "Even if it is *against* your wishes? We can take you away from Elliott, little human. After this judgment ends, there is a chance that you may never see him again..."

"May I be frank with you?"

Svetlana's expression changed. "I expect you to be."

"I have seen Elliott in fear of the vampire lord's wrath. I've seen how it drains him. It holds him back. In all my time with him, Elliott Craven has drilled into my head his apprehension of the *dreaded* vampire lords. The longer that he lives with that burden over his head, the harder it will be for him to become the lord he *needs* to be—the one that he *can* be. I don't know your intentions. For all that I know, you may conspire to destroy him after all. Maybe his fears were well placed... but, from my perspective, you already *had* your chance. You were *there.* All of you stood together on the Isle of Obsidian—with all the reason in the world to destroy Stonehold and Elliot along with it—but that's not what happened. You came in peace. You sat at his table and ate with him, and me, and it was one of the most fascinating moments of my life! If you meant to destroy him, that castle would already be smoldering ruins, and I'd be your prisoner."

"How do you know we haven't destroyed it in your wake?"

"Even if all seven of you could get on the same page, there's no way. You'd have finished what you started the day you arrived and gotten on with your *long* lives."

Svetlana's lips twitched; she burst into laughter.

"You may be naïve, but you are clever," she replied as she wiped a tear from her eye. "We've no intention to destroy Stronghold—it simply offers too much to the world right now..."

As her laughter subsided, she looked me straight in the eye. "But we *are* willing to depose an unfit ruler, if it comes down to that. How does that make you feel?"

I thought for a moment.

"You know his mother well. With all of her prestige in this world... if it was a unanimous choice to get rid of her only son, Elliott would've had to have done something to deserve it."

"You think he is capable of that?"

"I think everyone is," I answered. "When we feel like their backs are against the wall, we find ourselves willing to compromise on everything we stand for—in the name of what we *think* is right."

"A solid observation," she replied. "So, if we choose to take you away from Lord Craven..."

"You would be putting my back against the wall, and I'm not sure how I'd react to that... but I put my faith in you to make the right decision."

Svetlana appraised me with a long, lingering look. "Interesting," she finally said. "I believe you mean that."

I felt a wave of fatigue overcome me. It rose in the back of my head like a smothering sensation; my mouth went dry, and the world started to fade away.

"Ah. I wondered how long it might take."

"What's... happening to me?" I asked her.

"Lord Krum has explained all of this. Don't be afraid, Clara. You cannot resist his spell for long—only for moments at a time. Your sudden glimpses of awareness let us briefly study your *conscious* mind, and I've found this little conversation to be quite fascinating. Perhaps your frustrating resilience can be a proper tool…"

Everything grew hazy. "Am I… fading again?"

She nodded. "Sleep, Clara, and goodbye. I've learned *everything* I sought to understand."

CHAPTER 21
ELLIOTT

I t shouldn't have taken long for me to find Nikki Craven. All I had to do was track down the place in Stonehold Castle with the most horror among its citizens—where she was trying to use a poor spirit for target practice, or dueling half a dozen guards, or making some sort of bizarre threat against my people.

Surprisingly, this time was different. When I finally tracked her down, my sister was meditating on the edge of Craven Keep. Nikki was seated with folded knees, her eyes closed and breathing slow.

"There you are," I noted curiously.

She blinked open her eyes and glanced up to me.

"This is new," I observed. "What are you doing?"

"I've been reading in the libraries," she replied with a small smile. "I've taught myself a few techniques to soothe the madness inside me."

"Is it working?"

She leapt to her feet. "I've only just started…"

For a moment, the falling snow caught my gaze. An unnatural winter had descended upon Stonehold in the days after Clara Blackwell left our world through a spell of great, archaic power. The other holds suffered in unforeseen ways—nature itself seemed to have become unbalanced. I wondered what could be done to fix this.

"I have been thinking," I began.

"Me too," she rested against the stone teeth around the edge of the keep rooftop. "You go first."

"I think that I'm ready to entertain the notion that I made a few mistakes in Clara's absence... but I need your opinion and guidance, because you're the one who knows me best on this island."

She smiled in curiosity. "That's quite a change."

"What you said yesterday has had plenty of time to sink in. It's been all that I could think about all night—that, and my fear for that *insufferable* human's safety," I smiled confidently. The look faltered as my thoughts shifted. "I tried to be a good ruler. I really did. But I fell too far into darkness."

"I am familiar with darkness," my sister reminded. "It drenches me. It floods my blood in every minute of every day. I can feel it in my bones."

"How do you deal with it these days?"

"I have methods. They don't always work."

I nodded softly. "I want to help you."

"Help yourself first," she chided lightly. "You might forget, but I've been taking care of myself for a very long time now, Elliott."

"I haven't forgotten." I took her shoulders into my hands. "But I don't want you to have to face this alone. You came back to this island to help me—and the threat we feared has changed. The vampire lords are on our side, for the moment at least. My priorities are loosening up. It is long overdue that I focus on you, in any way that I can."

"Do you really mean that?"

I nodded tiredly. "I will try my best."

Nikki Craven took my face in her palms, earnestly staring deep into my eyes. "Elliott, my darling brother—more than ever, I truly, *sincerely* need you right now."

I sighed wearily. "There is so little of me to give."

She sisterly rested her forehead against mine for a moment, and then withdrew it. "Let me remind you of some of your recent victories, Elliott. You have returned to your home—this time, *with* your witch at hand. Your greatest regret has been undone. The enemies you have long feared now stand at your side. Your nemesis lies subdued and humiliated in your own castle dungeon. Brother, please forget about the human's trials for a moment: what more could you *possibly* need?"

I looked her in the eyes. "Nikki... am I truly a tyrant?"

Her brows furrowed in realization. "You really *have* been thinking this over, haven't you? It's eating away at you now; I can see it. I take it that you're finally ready to listen to reason..."

"We both know Clara was given that impression." I brushed away her hands. "Thanks to the interference of others in the castle, she apparently believes her time away twisted me into some kind of monster. Don't get me wrong: right now, my focus is not on them. At this point in time, my focus is better spent deducing whether or not they have an honest point. So, tell me: I am a tyrant?"

"No," she replied immediately.

"Good." I felt relief wash over me. "Because she—"

"But you *were* getting there."

"What?"

"I can't pretend otherwise. Clara's departure shoved you down a desolate path, Elliott. Your choices darkened by the day." She planted her hand on my shoulder. "For what it's worth, I firmly think that you were doing what needed to be done. But, as far as *tyranny* goes?" Her hand released its grip, and her flashed evilly. "Part of me kind of *really* enjoyed watching you in action."

I sighed. "That's the most damning evidence."

Nikki smirked. "Can't really argue with that."

"A tyrant," I shook my head in frustration. "Hard to accept. Harder still to understand how." My glance lifted to search her smirking expression. "I don't get it. If I had been shifting towards tyranny, why would you allow it? Wasn't protecting Stonehold the *entire reason* why you came back to the Isle of Obsidian?"

"Don't get me wrong. If you had *really* gone off the deep end I would have stepped in to resolve it... by any means necessary." Nikki hesitated for a moment. "Of course, it seems that precious little Kinsey was prepared to beat me to the punch. Credit where credit is due, that one really doesn't back down. She even tried to threaten *me* when I took the throne."

I snarled. "Kinsey..."

"But I can't blame her. Becoming a vassal gave her a real identity crisis. You've got to remember, she still takes the royal guard oath seriously, and they're clear on what to do if their liege is going off the deep end. The needs of Stonehold are greater than any vampire lord who seeks to rule."

"That's not her decision to make."

"She thinks it is."

"That guard is a traitor."

"That is a *dangerous* word to just throw around."

I cast her a furious look. "It was *her,* Nikki. *She* is the one who drove the wedge between me and Clara. I should have never let them be alone together—what is it with that girl and the bloody royal guards? They had *one* objective—keep the human safe—and they've failed me every damn time..."

Nikki listened to me rant, holding up one elbow and working her lower lip between her pinched fingers. As she silently watched my furious pacing, my little sister's eyes casually followed.

"What?" I finally snapped, throwing up my hands.

"Just thinking to myself."

"Care to share?"

"Well... it's just that you seemed to be making *such* good progress. It's a real shame to throw that all away, as soon as I mention her."

I glowered. "The vassal...?"

She shrugged, dropping her hands. "She's been scarce lately, hasn't she? For a sworn guardian, she's a terrible vassal."

"Fair point," I realized with annoyance.

"Here's a suggestion," Nikki noted. "Did you ever consider *asking* her what she wants from you? If you really wanted her on your side, you could have sat Kinsey down and apologized for your behaviour this past year. Seeing as she's so bent out of shape over it, that might go a long way..."

I steadily felt the fight in me shrivel. "Do you really think that would work?"

She smiled evilly. "Worth a shot. And hey, if Kinsey isn't

willing to change her tune, you could always have her *executed...*"

"*That* sounds more like you," I observed coolly.

Nikki shrugged, a devilish glint still in her eye. "Just an idea... but if I'm *really* your vassal again, I call dibs on giving her the killing stroke."

"We are not discussing you carving down my subjects," I told her sternly.

Is it too late to change Kinsey's mind? Could I seriously undo some of her antagonism by... talking to her?

"You're considering it," she smirked.

"I am."

"Good. I'll get the disemboweling knives ready."

"What? No, I meant that I'm considering *speaking* to her."

"Oh. Right." Nikki looked disappointed.

"It'll have to wait, though," I shook my head. "There is a much more pressing concern for this afternoon—we need to cross the ocean. Mattias Blackburn awaits."

"Ah yes," her eyes lit up. "I'd almost forgotten."

"Yes," I decided firmly, setting my jaw. "I think it's about time we finally find some overdue answers..."

CHAPTER 22
ELLIOTT

When we stepped through the portal beneath Blackburn Manor, Lord Mattias greeted us himself. Once we were reoriented, he turned and led us down the staircase.

"Welcome to Bleakwood, Lords Craven."

"Actually, just the one," Nikki chuckled impishly as we followed after him. "I have publicly given up my claim as vampire lord. I'm only here because you specifically wanted to talk to both of us."

"Is that so?" Lord Mattias turned to me.

"It is."

"Consider me surprised. I thought perhaps the two of you might leverage that particular advantage while it was still available. I cannot think of another time in our history that we've seen such a crisis over a throne."

I replied sternly. "We can't risk alienating the other lords at this critical juncture. Especially not while they hold Clara captive."

"Yet there are two of ascended blood in your hold."

"That was true even before Nikki undertook her ascendance," I reminded him. "Lorelei may have made herself unavailable, but her power was intact."

Mattias stiffened when I spoke my mother's name, but he didn't comment on it. Instead, he wordlessly led us through his own chrysm hub, teleporting us to one of the holding chambers and then escorting us towards his private study. I continued to speak as we walked.

"Nikki took over Stonehold during a time when I was gone from this world; she served on the throne, and has abdicated upon my return. The traditions are still being observed."

"I suppose that you may be correct," Lord Blackburn replied.

"Have you seen her yet?" I asked him suddenly, breaking this line of conversation.

"No. Clara will visit with me nearly last."

Nikki scratched her head as we stepped through the door to his study. "When she left, she went with Ooktuk Krum. Who came next?"

He held up a hand, motioning for us to shut up. It didn't take long to see why; the room was still occupied by a servant, stoking the fire.

"I can take it from here," the lord told him.

The servant nodded and climbed to his knees. After he returned his iron poker to the proper place, the lord paused him. "Wait." Mattias turned to us. "Would either of you like anything to drink? Something to eat?"

"I'll take tea," I replied coolly.

"Blood," Nikki grinned cheekily.

The vampire lord nodded, turning to the servant. "See that it is done. I'll take liquor. You know the kind."

"Of course, Lord Blackburn."

Once the room was ours, Mattias reverted his glare to us. "I am not meant to be discussing this with you."

"You are also not supposed to have invited us directly to your castle during the judgment," I replied, unimpressed. "Yet, you did so. We cannot influence the trial from outside, but it would give us solid peace of mind to understand it…"

Nikki shrugged. "I'm a *little* interested, I guess."

"Fine," I irritably corrected myself, rolling my eyes. "It would give *me* peace of mine…"

Lord Blackburn motioned for us to take the chairs by the roaring fireplace; he stayed standing, leaning his arm over the mantle and reflecting on the blazing glow of the embers.

"Lord Krum sent her to Lord Lovrić," Mattias spoke distantly. When he turned to us, the grave expression on his face didn't bode well. "There is already a problem. It started in Selvara Karn—and our friend Svetlana has since confirmed it."

My spirits crumbled. "What is it?"

"You *did* something to her, didn't you?" Nikki narrowed her eyes; her fingernails clenched into the surface of her armchair. "And I imagine that it's not exactly going to *plan*…"

Mattias nodded gravely. "That is correct."

"I knew it," I snarled. "Tell me, Mattias… how much of this *trial* was preconceived?"

"You misunderstand, Lord Craven"

Mattias turned from the mantle to face us, and the look on his glum face alarmed me. "There was a plan, but Lorelei's sudden passing changed everything. When your human made her decision to avoid our meeting, she opened the floodgates for a new possibility..."

"Lord Mattias... what have they done?"

"They cast a spell over her," he replied.

"*Which* spell?" Nikki gasped with delight. "Which spell was it?"

"Lord Krum was chosen to receive her first because the magic of his hold runs wild and rampant. The lords planned to do something dangerous, and they needed to ensure enough ambient magic to pull it off. They have chosen to examine the human when stripped of her mind. The spell they have cast is a powerful one—severing her personality, leaving behind what you might consider a *basic* version of self," he told us gravely. "For the moment, everything that makes Clara Blackwell who she is has been whisked away—the others want to study what kind of person is at the heart of her, rather than explore her ability to outwit or cater to them. They will judge Clara based on what they find in the *back* of her head."

A stunned silence fell over the room.

"They inhibited her?" Nikki asked, her joy suddenly shifting into fury.

"Thoroughly. She responds to questions and orders, but that is about as far as things go."

"So, what went wrong?" I inquired curiously.

Lord Blackburn smiled in dark satisfaction. "As it so turns out, your human is... more difficult than expected. It appears you might not have been lying to us when you explained her resistance to magic."

"She's fighting it," I realized. "And winning."

"Winning? No. Even she cannot help but fall before the

power of this magic... but she *is* doing the impossible. She has regained moments of lucidity. Ooktum had quite a difficult time keeping her suppressed, and Svetlana tells us that Clara regained her mind during *her* part of the trial. Each vampire lord has reinforced the spell in turn, but the fact that it even *requires* reinforcement is quite telling."

Nikki scratched her head. "So, what does that mean for Clara?"

Lord Mattias shrugged in nonchalance. "Clara was never meant to remember her experience in our castles. Clearly, that part of the trial is forfeit. For the moment, the lords are frustrated."

I narrowed my eyes. "Is Clara in any danger?"

"Lord Craven, Clara was in danger the very moment that she stepped foot upon this world." He shrugged again. "I believe that she will emerge from this trial unharmed. If what your mother told us really *is* true, Clara has a part to play in what is coming."

"What are you talking about?" Nikki asked darkly.

"The very reason I summoned you both," the lord of Bleakwood leaned back, tenting his fingers. "But first, allow me to remind you that the things you hear can never leave this room."

We both nodded in agreement.

The door opened; his servant had returned.

Nikki playfully swirled a wineglass of rich blood as I drank from my cup of tea. Meanwhile, Mattias sipped at a tumbler of amber liquid, compiling his thoughts.

"Lorelei Craven came to Bleakwood in her last days. While she was here, she did a great deal of studying in the vast libraries beneath Blackburn Manor. From what she discovered, and what she told the rest of the council, I have seen a colourful picture of events that came before... and those still to come..."

"Is this more about the Sanguine Ones?" I asked in a bored huff. "Because I've heard those stories before."

"The Sanguine Ones, yes," he agreed. "She went to look past the Pierced Veil several decades ago, and what she discovered changed her. It also inflicted a grave and terrifying punishment on her mind."

"The Pierced Veil?" I asked curiously.

"It is the jagged peak of the tallest mountain in our world, deep in a mountains of West Alevorra. The Pierced Veil is said to be the point where the realm is the thinnest, through which a powerful spell can be used to see beyond time and space. It is a grave taboo among the council to approach it, let alone use it for knowledge."

"Mum traveled there and used it?" Nikki asked. "Is *that* why she became so weird and aloof?"

"That was the curse."

Nikki and I shared a glance. I sighed, turning back to Mattias. "I think you should start at the beginning."

And he did.

For the next hour, Lord Mattias Blackburn told us a harrowing story of our mother—the woman who risked her life, her mind, and everything she had left to give to discover the answers to her suspicions.

He told us of her mental curse.

He told us of her fall from grace.

He told us of her knowledge of the Cataclysm.

And he told us of the Calamity yet to come.

CHAPTER 23
CLARA

I snapped awake to witness the open desert.

My upper body heaved as I dropped to the ground. The sensation overcame me as I uncontrollably let loose my stomach onto the sunbaked terrain.

"Took you long enough."

Wiping my lips, I shivered with discomfort. I lifted my head to see a sly, subtly mocking face, studded with bone piercings in the ears and through the nose. Short, crimson hair stuck out of her head in naturally spiky chunks, and her face was painted in angular swipes of dark red, tribal war paint.

"Lord Eyes-Like-Fire," I realized in awe.

"Not *lord*," she grumbled, reaching out her hand to pull me up. "Never cared for the title."

"Okay... Eyes-Like-Fire, then."

She smirked, roughly pulling me to my feet—and nearly wrenching my arm from the socket in the process. That's about when I realized that I wasn't wearing my Stoneholdian clothes; I was dressed in cut-off furs and tribal beads, as if I were a hunter of the plains.

"What's all this?"

The lord—not that I'd call her that again—laughed. "You will get used to that. When you entered my hold, we outfitted you more appropriately for your time here. You didn't argue when I suggested the attire of my people, so..."

"Wasn't I technically asleep or something?"

"I suppose," she shrugged. "We can continue with this discussion naked, if you'd prefer..."

I went red in the face. "Oh. That's not—I mean—"

Eyes-Like-Fire grinned wide enough that her fangs were visible. "Enough chatter. Now that you've rejoined me, human... I welcome you to the Twilight Gate."

I steadied myself against her and followed her gaze. Tall against the setting sun, I easily spotted it—standing here, alone in the desert, jutted a monolith of massive wooden timbers eight or nine stories tall. Perfectly flat in design, it ended in piercing peaks of wood shaved into round, jagged tips—like a gigantic fence gate standing on it's own.

The shadow it cast was monumental.

"What is that?" I asked. "Is that your castle?"

"In a sense," Eyes-Like-Fire replied calmly, watching my sense of wonder with faint amusement. "I like to spend my time away from there as often as I can."

"Why is that?"

She chuckled. "The vampire lords stay complacent. They may be content to spend their days in their castles, but not me. Nothing is better than the hot sun on your back, the camaraderie among your tribe, and the *thrill* of the hunt..."

Suddenly, her markings made sense.

"This is the Timberland Plains, right?"

Eyes-Like-Fire nodded. "Yes."

"On my world, this is a place called America. Before it was colonized by people from places you call Stonehold, the Falvian Badlands, and Alevorra, this hold ran free with a society that lived close to the earth. Dozens upon dozens of tribes lived by the hunt, praying to the very earth itself, and believed in honouring their kills. There were exceptions, of course—but it was a chaotic land that thrived in harmony with nature, taking, of course, but *always* giving back."

She watched me carefully, her eyes curious.

"I mean, I could be getting a lot of that wrong. I can tell you what they teach us in school."

"It's not quite the same here," the lord finally replied. "But it maybe close. The Timberland Plains are a wide and sprawling land of great majesty and powerful, roaming creatures. We hunt the beasts. We honour the beasts. Sometimes, the beasts hunt us back—but what better glory is there than to be locked in combat with a beast that could so easily slay you?"

I grinned. "Nikki would *love* you."

"Ah, yes—the one who was driven mad by magic. Is she a great warrior, the Craven girl?"

"You don't know the *half* of it."

Eyes-Like-Fire smiled warmly. "Then perhaps I was wasting my time on *you*, when I should have spent it on the warrior Craven. There is no better lust in this world than bloodlust. It drives me. It empowers me."

"That's why you stay away from the Twilight Gate?" I glanced back over my shoulder to the impressive wooden structure. "It's a nice castle, but I can imagine why you might feel trapped inside it…"

"Other cultures enjoy their vices. I enjoy the kill."

I glanced back. The vampire lord had since closed the distance between us—she stood so close that I could smell the dust her skin. In her burning gaze I could see the blaze of her soul. The spark that gave this lord life was something far more primal than what I'd seen in Stonehold or The Drenchlands—her eyes shined with something carnal, magnetic, and raw.

This lord was a warrior, through and through. It was a shame that I wouldn't remember seeing her in action. Seeing this lord snatch a spear and ride a tamed beast into battle would've made for an *amazing* experience.

"Your eyes really *are* like fire," I gasped.

"It is my spirit that burns," she smiled evilly.

She yanked me against her and held her fingers up to the setting sun. After they clicked, I heard the distant call of a great, roaring creature.

"I hope you are not afraid of Piasa birds."

I trembled. "That was a *bird?*"

Eyes-Like-Fire smirked. "This is going to be fun."

From the direction of the Twilight Gate whipped a silhouette against the setting sunlight. It fluttered high above, swooping in wide arcs, until it came roaring right towards us…

The creature snapped into position before us, first hanging aloft until landing on the baked terrain. I can only describe it like a large, flowing panther mixed with a grandiose hawk—almost a griffon, yet somehow nowhere near one. Before us, the Piasa bird sat tall and proud with a face half-feminine and half-beast, whipping her powerful serpentine tail around herself in the air. Her long body was covered in majestic feathers—the top layer were all brown like a standard hawk, but beneath it ran brilliant, glowing colours that gave the creature a royal presence. She stood on four claws and talons, and her gigantic pair of wings stiffly jutted up to the sky. Her head grew a bone headdress of antlers and feathers, giving way to long, flowing tufts of hair that rolled over her shoulders and partway down her giant back.

"That is the most *incredible thing* I have ever seen."

Eyes-Like-Fire smiled, lifting me onto the back of the creature as if I weighed nothing. The vampire lord climbed aboard ahead of me, soothing the Piasa bird with soft, loving noises and her hands along its feathers.

When she turned back, she grinned evilly.

"Poor little Clara... you haven't seen *anything*."

Before I could reply, we were off—I could hear my wailing screams as I clung on for dear life, and the tribal vampire lord of the Timberland Plains roared with her mocking laughter...

The beast flew with full confidence. The creature seemed to have complete dominion over the skies.

I felt myself lapsing in and out of awareness as we crossed the desert below. The radiant, cosmic night sky bathed us all in luminescent glow; I felt as if the stars themselves were twinkling just for us. Far below, when my mind let me focus on my surroundings, I could spot in the distance great herds of creatures that ran across the desert.

But we weren't over the desert anymore, I realized. I saw that we were flying over grasslands, and we lowered down onto the slight jutting hill of one above the endless green terrain. There, in the distance, I spotted the slightest hint of low mountains.

The vampire lord descended and helped me down from the Piasa. With a quiet, chittering screech into the creature's ear, she banished it away. My dazed eyes followed her as she then swooped high above the rolling prairies, lazily chasing after a nearby grazing herd for a quick, rejuvenating bite to eat.

"How long were we flying?" I asked.

Eyes-Like-Fire turned. "Oh, you're back again."

"Maybe I was here the whole time."

"No," she grinned derisively. "You weren't."

"It's all a bit of a blur…" I shook my head, trying to clear it. I already felt the sluggish draw of something heavy, pooling up from the cracks within my mind—I realized that, very soon, I would recede back into the confines of the spell.

"What do you think of my lands?"

I inhaled deeply and widened my eyes, as if trying to wake myself. My gaze took in the horizon, bathed in the crystal clear moonlight from above. I could see now that the grasses shimmered within the nocturnal glow. The rustling of a sweeping breeze through the countless acres of stalks released the slightest, trailing little bursts of twinkling dust into the moonlit air.

"There is nothing like this on my world. There may have been, once, but people have long since buried it under the footsteps of progress."

She didn't respond for a few moments. We watched as her Piasa cut down from the sky and made off with a small shape in the distance, clutched in her talons.

"You really *don't* have any magic on your world, do you,

Clara?" The vampire lord's eyes remained trained on the horizon, watching the creature in its great hunt. "Lord Craven spoke of the black night. It sounds dreadful to think of."

"It's beautiful in its own way," I replied sadly. "Outside of the city, you can pick out every single star."

She nodded softly.

"But you can *always* see the stars here," I told her. "Even in the height of the day, if you turn your eyes straight upward, they're there. That isn't the case on my world."

"What do you have during the day, then?"

"An ocean of the calmest blue, stretching from horizon to horizon. Then there are the clouds—big white puffs that can fill the sky, or hang low and pretty against a beautiful blue day. You can get lost in that sky, if you only lay back and appreciate it."

Eyes-Like-Fire nodded. "It is a shame none of us can see that. Your lord showed us his burns. He claims that the very light would incinerate us."

"Some of the most beautiful things kill."

The lord chuckled. "Yes. Such is true, even here."

It was growing harder to resist the pull in my head. I would disappear any moment now, sucked backwards into a robotic slumber until I snapped awake again, lost and disoriented in another hold.

I blurted: "Aren't you supposed to be judging me?"

Eyes-Like-Fire replied with a defiant, possibly even *amused* glare. "I don't really care about any of that. As far as I'm concerned, you are welcome part of this world, if you choose to be."

"Really?" I blinked in surprise. "Why is that?"

"You make Elliott happy," she replied simply. "And I doubt you're anywhere *near* the threat the others think you to be."

"They think I'm a threat?"

"Of course they do."

"But... how? Why?"

"Foolish questions demand foolish answers, Clara," the vampire lord warned me. "I think it is beneath you to insult my intelligence."

"I'm sorry. I didn't mean to. I'm getting tired again. It's getting harder for me to keep my head straight..."

"No worries," Eyes-Like-Fire replied as she held her fingers aloft, preparing to click them again and call back the Piasa. "I want to show you more of my hold."

"I'm not going to remember it."

"Who cares?" The lord grinned mockingly. "Maybe I just want to see it myself, and you're nothing more than a convenient excuse. Despite what you might think, the world doesn't revolve *around* you."

Her fingers clicked; the Piasa screeched distantly.

As the creature swooped up against the moon and whipped towards us, the sluggish void of life without awareness came roaring back. I'd held on for so long, but it was time for me to disappear back into nothingness.

The last thing that I saw, as the brilliant majesty of the Timberland Plains slipped away from all around me, was the smug and understanding smile of its tribal master.

CHAPTER 24
ELLIOTT

In the dead of the night, Stonehold Castle was always at its most silent. A ghastly quiet fell across the stronghold and made it unto a tomb.

I used to spend much of my time wandering these halls at night, didn't I? I reflected on what felt like simpler times. *When I needed to think, I'd wait until all the staff went to sleep, and I walked alone with my thoughts...*

There was certainly plenty to think about now, but I chose to not do that. Instead, I wandered through my castle in a simple, quiet, and nearly meditative daze.

And as I walked, I felt happier than I'd been in days.

The cold, crisp air of the Stoneholdian winter filled my senses as I ventured along covered walkways edging the servants' quarters of the castle. The filtered chrysm lighting of the recessed ceiling tiles held back the usual hellish glow, instead lighting my castle path with mild, yellowish-white brilliance. The lighting along the castle interiors was a nicety at best—all vampires could see in the dark, if they chose to do so…

I faintly heard a scraping sound echoing from far above. There, up near the edge of a distant roof, my sister was lazily draped against the edge while she sharpened yet another dagger with her whetstone.

For a moment, I thought about climbing up and discussing things with her. Something in the air sought to hold me back —it felt like the wrong decision to make.

I wondered for a moment, quietly watching her.

Sadistic and obfuscating at best, Nikki Craven could be a mystery at times. When this wild journey began, she was the first real ally I had on the island—if one were to not count our apathetic and borderline impartial mother, of course. It was our reunion that built the foundation that I stood on now, and I owed her a great debt.

I meant everything that I said to you. If there is a way to make you better… I want to be there for you.

She was unreliable sometimes, to be sure. Her grasp of her sanity was tenuous at best, even while she was on her *best* behaviour.

But above all that…

I loved my sister, and she loved me.

Together, we made a powerful pair…

Just not tonight, I thought to myself as I realized what needed to be done. I turned away from Nikki Craven and made my way towards a distant servant, determined to track down the whereabouts of the one I needed to find.

❧

I SAW HER SEATED ON THE EDGE OF A PAVILION IN THE GARDENS. The guard stared at the stars; her shoulder was slumped against the wall, and she lightly kicked her feet off the brink of the platform.

For a moment, I thought about leaving her alone, but my boots moved without me. Soon I was at her side and following her gaze.

"Lord Elliott," Kinsey dryly observed. The contempt in her voice was palpable, but I overlooked it for the sake of a productive reunion.

"Walk with me," I requested, "if you would."

She glanced up. "Are you giving me an order?"

Her tone was agreeable; the intent was combative.

"I am not," I replied calmly. "I merely wished to talk."

"Oh." She looked once more to the radiant stars. "I think I am fine right here. But thanks for the offer."

Disappointed clouded me, but I was determined not to hold this against her. *Perhaps I was wrong,* I thought. *Perhaps the point of no return has already come; she might not be willing to entertain reconciliation any further.*

"Enjoy your evening," I responded before leaving.

Instead of venturing back into the castle, I chose to walk among the royal gardens. *I never spent much time in them,* I reasoned; *certainly, I can spare a few minutes, now more than ever. You have now become a memorial to more than just Fiona Craven, haven't you? You carry the blood of two vampire lords—mother and daughter...*

I thought to the revelations of Mattias Blackburn.

In his words, you never stopped fighting for us. While your mind slowly decayed in your skull, you did everything in your power to equip us for what comes next...

*You really **were** always on our side.*

And I'm so sorry that I never took time to appreciate that.

Sinking to a knee in front of a prominent rosebush, I bowed my head in pained grief and loss.

I loved my mother as I'd loved my older sister. Both of these powerful women in my life had shown me what it meant to be strong—to be unbending in spirit, and to be a fighter until the end. Lorelei Craven battled mostly with her mind and her convictions; in contrast, Fiona was one to solve her problems with her fists.

Nikki was right, and I'd known it at the time.

We were all we really had left in this world.

Regardless of the fate of Clara Blackwell, the entire Craven family was falling apart at the seams. Nikki and I stood in the ashes of the dying dynasty, upon a pillar of legacy that steadily crumbled—like disintegrating stone against a mighty wind. No matter where I turned, no matter how I fought, it felt as if the monumental gifts of Lorelei Craven would fade away to nothing in our grasp.

If either or both of us died, there would be nobody else to continue the bloodline. Our beloved Stonehold would shrivel on the vine and die in our wake.

I must do right by you, I whispered in my head. *There has to be a pivot here—if I want to rise to your memory and fulfill my duty, I must become something better than I now am. I must fashion myself into a true leader—no more hate and no more excuses.*

Opening my eyes, I straightened my back and rose to my feet, taking note of my vassal's approach.

"I see that you changed your mind."

"As much as I love the stars," Kinsey observed, "they will

still be here tomorrow. I can stargaze later. For now, maybe a walk won't kill me."

I hid a smile.

ॐ

KINSEY FELL INTO STEP BESIDE ME AS WE GRADUALLY VENTURED further into Lorelei's gardens. She chose to remain silent as we wordlessly admired the beautiful flowers beneath the endless frost.

"I don't have any idea of how much longer they can last like this," I thought aloud. "There is powerful magic woven into these gardens, but I'm not certain if it was ever meant to withstand something like this winter."

"Do you know how to stop it?" She asked quietly.

"It had something to do with Clara leaving. I hoped bringing her back would undo the damage, but there is still snow in the air. I may have to consult Lord Lovrić for help."

"The other holds have their own problems," Kinsey reminded me. "Disasters have ravaged the whole world for the past year. But they did seem oddly peaceful while they were here—maybe things have improved in their holds. Who's to say?" She shrugged noncommittally.

As she spoke, I started to carefully consider how to broach the subject. But my companion clearly had other plans, because she paused me with a splayed hand to my chest and a glare on her face.

"Your speech…"

I lifted my chin, gazing sorrowfully into her eyes.

"Did you really mean what you said?"

"I've been thinking deeply about this. For some time, I was

beginning to consider you an enemy… but I can see that I was mistaken."

"I am an enemy only to those who threaten the safety of our realm," Kinsey replied sternly. "But… I'm willing to admit that people can change, and that I can be mistaken in my own judgement. If your intentions are pure, I believe that they can draw Stonehold back into the light…"

"I need your help," I conceded to her.

"My help?"

"I find myself increasingly broken, and I'm trying to pull myself back from the shattered remnants. I can *be* the ruler Stonehold requires—but I need the counsel and help of those who believe in this place… those who are willing to do what *must* be done, even if it means opposing me when I stray from the right path."

Conflict hid behind her otherwise blank expression. I didn't need the presence of Clara Blackwell to help me read the anguish of the torn guard.

"You broke my heart, you know," she told me.

I blinked. "You… loved me?"

Kinsey snorted. "What? Get over yourself. No, not like *that*…" Shaking her head, she took a deep sigh. "No. I pledged my *life* to you, Lord Elliott. I swore an oath to protect and defend you until my dying breath…"

She jammed her finger into my chest.

"You *broke* your side of the oath. When you slid into darkness, you betrayed everything good about yourself; you betrayed your subjects, whom you were bound into duty to honour and serve. You betrayed *me*, after I made it my life's mission to protect you."

"I made decisions that were necessary for the security of the hold…"

"You didn't trust me to understand that. You kept me in the dark," she replied.

Kinsey never looked more vulnerable than she did at this moment, not even the first time I'd gone to visit her in a medical bay bed—right after the tatzelwurm attack.

"I was supposed to be your guardian, Lord Elliott—*you* were supposed to be my liege. But how can I serve and protect you when I question all that you do? When your actions seem to betray the safety and goodwill of your people, how am I supposed to stand by and abide that?"

"You have put a lot of thought into this," I said.

"Yes," she noted penitently. "I have."

"Lots of long and sleepless nights, I imagine."

"More than you know, I'm sure."

"I understand that you have struggled to reconcile your allegiance to me with the oaths you took as a royal guard… and I sympathize. Allow me a chance to prove that I am a leader you can proudly serve."

In near resignation, she searched my gaze.

"I mean it," I reiterated firmly. "I need all the allies I can get in whatever comes next. You have proven to me that you're a capable warrior, a dedicated guardian, and a valuable advisor. Serve me again as my vassal. Stand by my side and help me forge the way forward."

She didn't answer immediately—the guard dwelled thoughtfully for a sparing few seconds.

"If I do this," she finally replied, "I cannot promise that I will agree with every path you walk… nor will I offer any apologies to your human, or to you, should I disagree with your choices."

I nodded gravely. "I only ask for a clean slate," I said. "But you must be willing to give me the same. My end of this bargain will be upheld. But you must not antagonize Clara or work to undermine me from the shadows. I expect you to approach me directly with any grievances you may have. I do not ask for subservience, but I do require loyalty... and it will be rewarded in kind."

Kinsey paused. I considered that she might renege on the terms after all, but she took a knee before me and lowered her head. "We have a deal, Lord Craven. I shall stay your vassal, and your protector."

I motioned for her to rise. "In that case, call me Elliott."

"Very well then," she replied. "*Elliott.*"

This time, I didn't hide my smile.

CHAPTER 25
CLARA

I snapped awake in a quick fit.

"My word!" A vampire masseuse staggered back.

Light and airy laughter came from the nearby table. When I turned, the vampire lord Chanda Song rested on her stomach with her face against her folded arms. Over her slender curves, a long white towel draped—the same kind that covered me.

"Why am I naked!" I gasped, embarrassed.

"It's called a *massage,* darling," the young, beautiful vampire sweetly smiled my way. "You arrived in such utterly *frazzled* condition. I take it that our tribal friend did a number on you…"

I tried to remember. It was like a distant dream.

The distant flight came to mind, and my eyes flew open. "There was an incredible bird…"

"She took you on the Piasa?" Chanda Song laughed in that soothing, melodic tone of hers. "Well, *no wonder* you were so exhausted! I'm a little jealous—she doesn't like to let *anyone* ride her precious beast..."

Was that true? I thought on that for a moment.

"I thought I'd get to know you through a day of rest and relaxation! You certainly looked like you needed it and I'm *always* in the mood for taking a moment away from the world..."

"Well, I appreciate that," I laughed awkwardly.

"Good! Then settle back down and let my girl work her magic. I swear you'll feel like a new woman."

I followed her advice and relaxed back against the massage table. As I felt the masseuse's hands work their way back onto my body, I took in my new surroundings.

We were in an open veranda atop a stone structure of some kind—a temple, perhaps? The taut red covering above us blocked out the bright sunlight and made our relaxation area a makeshift tent. In the distance ahead, tropical trees flourished and several colourful birds flitted between them.

These thoughts quickly receded—but this time, it didn't have anything to do with being pulled back under a formidable amnesia spell. My attendant's strong and capable hands worked out a tough knot I didn't realize I had, focusing just beneath my right shoulder blade before running her immensely powerful fingertips up and down the edges of my spine in slow kneading motions. I felt all my stresses melt away as she worked. For every single, tiny ounce of pain I endured under her pressure, I received double the sensation in raw pleasure.

"Feels great, doesn't it?" Lord Song asked chirpily.

"It... honestly does. I can barely think!"

"That's my girl," she smirked, glancing up from her forearms to my masseuse. "When I told you to relax and let her work her magic, that wasn't a figure of speech..."

"No kidding," I murmured.

The masseuse lowered the towel further and began peppering my back with the sides of her hands. I felt my entire body rattle under the assault, but it felt much too good to stop her.

The vampire lord and I let our attendants massage us both away to a place of untold satisfaction—and the whole world melted away... but not in the way the spell drew me from my body. This was pure relaxation of a physical nature... and I knew that I would remember every fleeting moment.

⚜

ONCE OUR ATTENDANTS FINISHED THEIR WORK, LORD SONG and I rose from the table and redressed. She had chosen a pair of summer dresses for us—hers was a simpler one with a soft, gentle mint green tone that accentuated her golden hair, whereas mine was a bold, shorter plum and black-trimmed ensemble that worked to properly highlight my figure and dark hair. *I've never worn anything like this,* I realized with a warm smile. *But I suppose the same could be said about most of the things I've woken up in this week...* I glanced over to her as she adjusted her jewelry in a hand mirror. I saw how her beautiful garment stretched down to her shins and flowed softly over her pale forearms.

"Do you like it?" Lord Song asked happily, eying me through the hand mirror.

"I do. It looks great on you."

"Oh, I wasn't talking about *me*, silly. Yours!"

I did a little twirl in my dress. The bottom flared in a poof of black netting that felt like how delicious candy *tasted* against my skin. I found myself adoring this dress more and more.

I beamed in astonished delight. "You know, I think this dress is the most beautiful thing I've ever worn!"

"Really?" The vampire lord finished fiddling with her ear, turning over her shoulder with a disappointed look. "That's such a simple piece! I'll suppose I'll have to have a terse word with that *Elliott* of yours..."

"He has plenty of beautiful things for me to wear."

Lord Song stepped across to me and put her hand on her hip, lightly swaying in her figure. In the same flip of the coin, the vampire lord of Alevorra looked both mischievously youthful and deeply matronly.

"*Beautiful* doesn't cut it. Upon this world, you are a dazzling gem—and you should be treated as such!"

"Oh, I'm not all that..."

"Nonsense!" The gleaming, cheerful look in her eyes made me think, for the most fleeting of moments, that I was her best friend in the world. "Beauty is all too common. You are *rare*. Don't let anyone make you forget it. You're a human—an *actual, live human!* Your mere presence sets my senses wild. Every color is more vivid... every scent more incredible."

"Lord Song," I replied, changing the subject, "I was led to believe you were meant to test me when I was *unaware*... but I feel very much awake."

The vampire lord grinned. "*Everything* is a test, my darling. Even the most lackadaisical and carefree among us are watching your every move—and hanging on your every word..."

My expression must have faltered, because the fair vampire lord lit up her eyes in kind amusement. "Oh, no reason to be *too* alarmed, Clara. We don't honestly think that you *intended* to subvert our wishes with your surprising resistance the suppression of your mind... although, it *does* make studying you a great deal more difficult than expected..."

It shouldn't have surprised me that she might be so forthcoming with that information. A part of me really believed that this lord, above all the others, truly wished to get to know me. In another lifetime on another world, I could see us growing up together... almost...

"I wish I could do something about that," I shrugged offhandedly. "At this point, I'm a passenger to whatever's going on. Not that I mind, I guess, but it's strange to find yourself jumping from one place to the next with no memories in between. It feels like all I've got are photographs of my experiences. They're like fresh snapshots in my mind—something to remember you by."

She tilted her head. "What's a snapshot?"

"It's an image, captured with a..."

Lord Song hung on my every word.

"Maybe *painting* is a better term here."

"This 'snapshot' is a technology on your world?"

I nodded absentmindedly; I privately thought back to how strange it was to not have a smartphone on me. Elliott's world was so bizarre and unique that I rarely missed it—but having one in my hands would make answering Chanda's questions so much easier.

"All of our phones have cameras." I tried to explain.

"Phones?"

"A handheld device that can communicate over long

distances… you speak into it and another person can hear you on their phone. It does so much more though…"

"Like these snapshots?" Chanda asked.

"Yes, pictures, and you can even take pictures that move, preserving memories crisper than a dream. Most people my age use their phones for a kind of ongoing popularity contest —but you can still… oh, I've already lost you, haven't I?"

Lord Song gave a confused, sly smile. "I understood some what you've said. Why did your people create such wondrous devices?"

"My world doesn't have magic. We can't cast ourselves halfway across the world with a chrysm node, or put someone under an amnesia spell, or live a thousand years…"

She nodded, aware of all of this.

"…But we make up for our limitations with technology. We cross oceans in giant metal machines that carry hundreds of humans across the sky. We have cameras that can cast our image round the world in an instant. Humans are capable of incredible destruction, but we also do wonderful things. We walked on the moon. We can—"

"Wait a minute there. Did you just say that humans have been on the *moon?*"

We glanced up to the sky. Even during daylight, the stars were visible—but there was no moon just yet.

"Okay, pretend the moon is there," she laughed.

"Yeah, humans have been to the moon."

"A *lot* of them?"

"Only a few. I don't actually know the exact number. Perhaps a dozen or more. We built enormous rockets that reached beyond the sky. They even sent back moving pictures for us to watch. I wish I could show them to you! We haven't been back to the moon in many years now. Our world leaders have been focusing on matters closer to home..."

"Can you tell me how these rockets set forth from the ground?" Chanda asked with great interest.

"They rise on a column of fire... but I don't really have the answers you're looking for. I'm not exactly a rocket scientist..." I replied.

Lord Song started talking about space, but I started to feel woozy. Needing to rest for a minute, I pressed my shoulder up against a stone pillar. *It's coming again. This time, I feel a little faint in the head...*

"Oh, you're leaving now, aren't you?"

I glanced up at the disappointed expression in Lord Song's face, and I nodded weakly. "I think so."

Chanda Song smiled, but I was unable to reply. Already I could feel my rapid slide back into the darkness.

The vampire lord slipped her pale arm around me. "Clara Blackwell... it was fun while it lasted, wasn't it? I'll be seeing you again soon..." Her sparkling eyes flashed impishly for a brief moment. "For now, please send my very best to Lord Blackburn..."

CHAPTER 26
AKACHI

Powerless.

It took me so long to think of the word.

In this place, I felt *powerless*—and I **hated** it.

I could barely remember how I'd even gotten to this accursed meadow, nor did I know how long I had been here. My great strength was sapped, and the cane at my hand served a greater purpose than had been intended. As a result, I bitterly wandered around lush trees and babbling brooks, loathing all of its pastoral bliss with the full intensity of my being.

Everything felt… *off,* somehow.

I could only remember a few minutes at a time.

It struck me that I was walking through, not quite a meadow, but the memory of one. Everything I saw from the corners of my tired eyes was hazy and incoherent at best, but it snapped into place with direct scrutiny. The place felt like an infernal prison. Despite my best efforts to walk a straight line, I was wandering this damned place in circles. Time meant nothing here, at least not to me.

All of this frustrated me to no end.

There came a moment when I realized I was not alone. Standing in the distance between the trees a dark, hooded woman was watching me—and she had been for some time.

She seemed vaguely familiar.

"If you have *anything to do* with why I'm here, I will personally rip out your throat," I hissed venomously at the warden to my prison.

I could not see her face.

But I *felt* that she smiled.

It made me hate her even more.

When I finally drew near, the woman responded. "Welcome, Lord Akachi. I see you've finally made it."

"Finally? I've been here for *ages*."

"*Ages* is relative, my lord. It took you a while to find your way, yes, but you've only been walking for a few short days. I am astonished at your blindness—I've been more patient than I think you appreciate."

"What am I doing here?" I demanded.

"Your enemies have been foolish and zealous," she replied, "and they have overestimated their strength. In their hubris, they bound you within a place that bore a very powerful death, where *I* could reach you."

"I know you," I realized.

"I would be offended if you didn't."

"But I thought you—"

"It matters not," the hooded woman sharply cut me off. "You have wasted your time here, feebly wandering like the old, weakened man you truly are."

"I am a vampire lord," I bowed my chest. "I am one of the most powerful creatures alive, and I maintain the position through sheer strength and cunning. How daring you are to insult me," I smirked deviously.

"How *little* your strength matters here."

The smirk left my face. "You affront me."

"In the grand scheme of things, my lord, you mean startlingly little," she replied offhandedly. "But I have come, and I have patiently waited, so that I might speak with you in private."

"For what purpose?" I narrowed my eyes.

"You crave power," she noted. "I offer it."

"Power." I bitterly balked. "*What* power?"

Although I couldn't see this, I felt the woman smile once more. "My master has taken me as a vessel beyond the veil, but requires another on the *physical* plane. You have been made vulnerable at a time that serves him. If you were to pledge him your undying allegiance, you would be granted considerable magic to wield."

"Magic? I already *have* considerable magic."

"No. You have natural talents that are enhanced by the blood in your veins. What you are now being offered is beyond such limitations. Imagine, Lord Akachi, what a vampire lord of your stature could accomplish—with powers that rival the world's *greatest* spell-casters..."

My eyebrow arched. "Oh?"

"You would become unstoppable."

"They already stopped me," I replied testily, snatching at distant memories of the events that had placed me here.

"Yes. You know them now for their disloyalty. I cannot imagine you would abide a second betrayal," she reflected with a conniving tone. "Consider, Lord Akachi, what could be done against the vampire lords if you were made truly capable of *punishing* them…"

"That is a compelling possibility. But I do not live to *serve* —not the other vampire lords, not *you*, and certainly not this *master* of yours."

"He does not require much."

"The fact that he requires *anything at all* is already too much," I stated firmly.

"You would turn down the opportunity?"

"What happens if I do?"

She shrugged. "You will stay here, left to the mercy and whim of your opponents. They exact their wishes against you, and you suffer them without a course of retaliation."

"I am the ruler of the Falvian Badlands. Don't make the mistake that so many have of underestimating me. My *retaliation* will come swift, strict, and fierce."

"And meaningless," she observed.

"It is my choice. I am a proud and willful vampire, and I shall not bend to the whims of another. That is my final response, both to you and *whomever* you serve."

The woman nodded. "Such is your choice, yes."

"You have no power over me."

"That is not chiefly true," she replied darkly. "Your contribution was preordained the moment you stepped foot in this place—and your consent is unnecessary. All that changes, Lord Akachi, is that you will have a smaller role to play in the festivities to come. When you think back on this moment, remember that you rejected an honored seat at the table…"

She pulled her hood back, revealing a youthful face that smiled wickedly. "Goodbye, Lord Akachi."

Constraining vines whipped up from the meadow ground and bound me at my wrists. I snarled as they forced me down onto my knees; in terror, I saw how the grasses writhed, as if a thousand things slithered below them. "What is the meaning of this?"

"I warned you. I cannot be held accountable now."

"You warned me of *nothing!*"

"The reason it took you so long to see me is that you are oblivious," she spoke serenely. "I have been warning you all this time, and still you defy us. Now, you will pay the price. You have something that we need, you foolish old man, and if you will not give it freely, we shall take it."

She placed her hands on my forehead as the growth began to swarm around me. I was held fast in place, feeling my control over this strange dream being wrenched away in a powerful rage.

I opened my mouth to scream.

But it was too late.

CHAPTER 27
CLARA

The first thing I realized was that I was choking.

I was pulled up from my seat by a strong presence; I felt it perform a variant of the Heimlich maneuver on me, and I hacked up a piece of partially chewed food. After I quickly coughed up a storm, the unseen presence very carefully lowered me back into my chair.

My blurry, wet eyes couldn't focus on anything else around me. I tried to sniff away my running eyes, just as the entity handed me a napkin.

"Thank you," I choked out.

"You picked a poor moment to awaken."

I dabbed at my eyes and blew my nose. As I looked up at the figure, I saw that he was some sort of a guard. He took his position back against the wall, and I glanced down at my clothing this time—a pleasant gown of cute colours and flattering curves.

I let my gaze take in my surroundings.

I sat in a stately dining hall of dark, polished wood, immaculately decorated in a regal setting. A modest, small feast was set before me, with enough food for at least two— but I was the only one at the table. I realized that a half-eaten plate was at my seat to the left, which was the head of the arrangement. My eyes moved away to take in the greater environment. Elegant décor of all sorts was carefully arranged along the walls and upon rigid bookcases. Whoever this belonged to was a person of great taste.

One piece of art in particular caught my eye—it was a large painting mounted down to the right. Standing in a snowy forest was some sort of a large, wide-faced wolf in glowing white fur on massive paws. It was meant to look like a wolf, but something about it told me that it was a great deal worse than that.

So distracted was I by the painting that I rose from my seat, wandering over to look at it. I did not notice the presence of the vampire lord who had silently appeared in a doorway, watching me.

I stood in front of the painting and tilted my head. The fierce look in the creature's supernatural eyes called to me somehow. One look in that fiery gaze and I knew the truth: this thing was a hunter of the highest malice.

"Waheela," a timbered voice muttered from across the room. I turned sharply. Standing at the edge of the dining hall and quietly observing me was the powerful shape of a vampire lord with graying hair. I searched my memory for his name: *Lord Mattias Blackburn.*

"Waheela," I repeated with a nod, turning back to it. "This creature knows no mercy."

"That is correct," Lord Blackburn noted dryly. "The Waheelas stalk the forests of Bleakwood like few others, choosing and killing the largest prey that they can find."

"How do they kill? Like a wolf?"

"Yes," he replied, "with a mild caveat. *Decapitation.* They treat it like a hobby. Nobody really knows why."

I shuddered. "They just... *sever* heads for fun?"

"They are further out west, in a land that has come to be called the Headless Valley. Their only saving grace is that they hunt in solitude. Waheelas are lone wolves, you see. They don't tend to get along..."

The lord took his place at the table, and I cleared my head of the horrible creature and joined him.

"To state the obvious, you are awake."

I nodded passively, eying my food.

"Do you not like it?"

"I can't answer that honestly. Coming back made me... choke on it. The timing was a little off there, I guess." When I glanced up at him and saw his quiet expression, I quickly added: "But I'm certain it was wonderful."

The vampire lord nearly smiled. "Apologies. There's never any telling when you're going to snap back to us."

"Tell me about it," I smirked.

The vampire lord sighed lightly as he glanced down at my plate. "I imagine you won't be touching much more of that. Fancy a walk?"

"Do I have the time before I go?"

He chuckled. "Probably not. Let's find out."

At the lord's behest, he reintroduced me to his personal castle—Blackburn Manor.

Having *manor* in the name did little to explain the sheer scale of the vampire lord's personal home. Every corner that we turned seemed to offer another twisting hallway; every door we passed through offered another grand chamber, filled with decorum.

It struck me then just how very *different* the castles of the vampire lords were. No two of them were quite anything like the others. They were perfectly indicative of their holds and their masters—and what *this* lair told me about Lord Blackwood was that he was a rigid man who delighted in the finer things in life.

He was a classy lord, and his home reflected that.

This manor was built from tip to tip with gleaming, dark wood, treated and scrubbed and allowed to breathe out its rich, chocolate midnight hues. Blackburn Manor was the most sophisticated evolution on the simple log cabin that I had ever encountered, and something about the natural components enriched me. I could just nearly smell the musk of the thick wood as I drew closer to the walls, peering between the mounted decoration plates, or the beautiful paintings that the lord collected.

Our path occasionally took us outside a wing, along the outer edges of the manor. The cold, crisp air sucked into my lungs as I stared out over the tundra valley that stretched in all directions; a frozen lake sprawled out to the front of the stately manor, at least a mile across in any directions.

The lord turned to me, sipping his blood. "So, Clara, what do you think of my castle?"

"It's marvelous," I offered him. When he didn't care to reply, I continued. "It's got *manor* in the name, but it's a lot more like a wooden palace than a mere manor. How long ago was this built?"

"There's no telling," Lord Blackburn responded. His icy cool glance slid across the surrounding frigid lands, from the staggering ice caps down to the chilly forests. "The castles of the vampire lords are all places of power, you see. These structures precede our families. Some theorize they are the legacy of the Sanguine Ones, but most believe that those creatures never existed…"

"I think I remember Lorelei mentioning them at some point," I told him.

Lord Blackburn's expression went stone cold in an instant. At the time, I barely noticed. "Yes, I imagine so. She was always going on about the old fables—*that one* in particular was a rather common topic of hers."

We stared over the ice for a moment longer before I was too cold to withstand it. I followed the vampire lord of Bleakwood inside, blowing on my frozen fingers until they heated back up.

"How have I been doing so far?" I asked coyly.

"You mean, with the Council of the Eight Holds?"

I nodded vigorously, trying to rub the last little bits of warmth back into my hands. "It feels like I am catapulting from one of you to the other with no time in between. I feel as if I've only been away from Stonehold for an hour or two at most."

"You've been gone for five days."

I sighed at that answer and gave up on my prickling cold

hands. They were just going to have to *stay* cold for the moment.

Lord Mattias took a sip of his blood again.

"The others have rather mixed opinions of you. You have been doing rather well when you're cognizant, but that is not what they're examining you for. The vampire lords are more worried with your innate qualities."

"You say that as if you are not testing me."

"I'm not," he replied offhandedly.

"You've already made your decision?"

Lord Blackburn nodded—and I sensed a great deal of sadness well up within him. "Lorelei Craven would've wanted you to be united and safe at Elliot's side. It is in her honour that I cast my vote to protect you."

"In her honour?" I grinned. "You say that as if she, well…"

The lord's gaze averted away.

Panic gripped. "Lord Blackburn? What are you…?"

"Mattias," he cut me off. "Simply Mattias."

I swallowed fearfully. "Mattias… are you telling me that something *happened* to Lorelei?"

When he set his jaw, I had my answer.

"No," I whispered. "But how?"

"She did it to herself," he replied gravely.

I held my hand to my chest in shock. The matron to the Craven household had been kind to me—mostly. She was a little hard to grasp at times, but she was intensely prideful and, when the fancy struck her, she was kind.

"Lorelei Craven broke our taboos to see *beyond* the world," he told me firmly. "There is a penalty to this, and a reason why the vampire lords forbid it. She insists that she saw visions through the veil. But her punishment for this sacrilegious act was to be stricken with a *powerful* curse, an affliction that slowly sapped her of her mind and spirit. It's been eating at her for decades, and her increased reliance on magic rapidly sped up the curse."

"And her... departure?" I asked as tenderly as I could. "Was there some catalyst?"

"When the vampire lords came, she faced off against Lord Akachi Azuzi." Lord Mattias glanced away with a pitiable look of penitence. "Their battle required the rest of her strength, and the curse destroyed what was left of her."

I trembled with grief. "How did she go?"

"The way she would have wanted," Mattias told me. "She died in her gardens, staring upon the stars. By then, her memories were gone. She could not remember who she was, who *I* was, or whom Fiona Craven was... all of it had been taken from her. Her memories left her, and she faded away until there was nothing left."

"That's... *horrible*," I held back tears.

"As the death of vampire lords go, it was the most peaceful passing in recorded history." He lowered his eyes, and I could see the slightest hint of a tear. "We are brought into a world meant for violence and chaos, and we leave this world in violent ways. It is against our nature to keep the peace across the holds. In recent years we endeavor to fight against our *base* instincts. That is why the lords rebelled against the dark ambitions of Lord Akachi Azuzi—he who meant to betray the peace, and therefore... the fragile balance. Even so, it is unlikely that I will live long enough to succumb to old age. The life of a vampire lord is a dangerous one."

I nodded remorsefully. "A magical curse explains a great deal about Elliott's mother. I never knew what she was thinking, and she seemed inconsistent in the times I encountered her."

"She struggled to manage her mind, yes. But the moment that she chose to pay the price, her fate was irrevocably sealed." Even as he averted his eyes, Mattias could not hide his despair. "Lorelei Craven is no more."

"I don't understand. They knew for an entire day?" I shook my head in mounting confusion. "Why couldn't Elliott tell me this? Why didn't Nikki? Why am I hearing this from you?"

"As I recall, you were being... difficult," he cast me a small appraising glare. "Perhaps *that* had something to do with it."

"This is huge, though... even if he were mad at me, I don't see why he couldn't have just told me."

"Why do you think you have that entitlement?"

I glanced up at Lord Blackburn. "Huh?"

"Tell me, little Clara Blackwell," Mattias responded coolly, swirling his glass of red in his hand. "Do you presume to understand the depths of his motivations? Where do you draw the conclusion that you know better than he?"

I didn't immediately have an answer.

"While you might be acquainted with his burdens, Elliott Craven has been saddled with far more than you could fathom. He does not understand his fate in the events to come —and I'm afraid he has only come *this* far due to blind luck and a world that has, thus far, openly favoured him. Lorelei believed that you have been bound together into something that defies explanation. She spoke of something powerful in the shadows—a great menace that stirs from far beyond our sight. If the crazed murmurings of that woman are to be believed at face value... we could all be in grave danger, and the strength of your connection with Elliot cannot be compromised."

"But... Lorelei..." I began, only to be cut off by Mattias's strong voice.

"Lorelei Craven is gone. Beyond the help of his unreliable and darkly twisted sister, Elliott is alone... now more than ever. He is going to *need* you, Clara. If you are unwilling to play your part in the face of this impending storm, then he is going to need someone *else*."

I sighed. It was exactly what I knew that I needed to hear, even if I knew I didn't want to. "I can't just change who I am... or the ways that I feel."

"Of course you can't. I am certainly not asking you to," he replied softly. The vampire lord placed a warm, strong hand against my shoulder. "I am only asking you to keep an open mind about Elliot's choices—*especially* if a future with that man is what you desire. Elliott is flawed. So are *you*. Both of you must take great strides to face the future together..."

"Yeah," I conceded. "I guess that we do."

"You are a willful creature," he remarked. "All of us can see that. The others have specifically commented on your stubbornness, among your *other* traits..."

"What other traits?" I asked.

He smiled knowingly.

"I know, *I know...* I can't know. That's okay."

Mattias nodded to himself. "A wise choice. It is best to not preoccupy yourself with these things, Clara. You have come so far, and you have so far yet to go. Lord Vasiliev awaits. It's a shame you cannot be more adequately prepared for that one..."

"I think I'll manage her."

Lord Blackburn nodded sagely. "I think you might be right —and I believe you're about to find out, either way…"

"What do you mean?" I asked.

But I already understood as the world began to drift away… after all, I'd been fighting the darkness for the last handful of minutes…

CHAPTER 28
PETER

I checked my wounds in the cell mirror.

The beatings had stopped when Vera Partridge realized I had given them all that I knew. From my perspective, it seemed I had very little to offer.

At least *now* I was given four walls with a tired old cot and a functioning toilet. For the first few days, I would always have to *beg* to be allowed a moment to relieve myself. They would ignore any of my complaints about the fluorescent lights overhead, and how hard it was to get even half an hour of sleep against them.

This cell didn't even *have* a light... not that I was complaining. It had a small window, so at least I could keep track of the passage of time.

It was the simple things in life, really.

THEY'D LEFT ME IN THERE A FEW DAYS BEFORE I HEARD A knocking at my door.

"Don't come in, I'm not decent!"

The door unlocked and Vera Partridge entered with an amused grimace on her face. "I see that you've retained your sense of humor, Peter."

"Nothing in here to sharpen but my wit," I said.

"Isn't that the truth..." She glanced around the four walls of my meager cell. "Listen, Peter... I can see that we've been a bit *naughty* in our treatment of you so far. It doesn't suit you to live like a prisoner, does it?"

"I mean, I'd complain, but I don't want to go back to the interrogation room. I've noticed that my complaints seem to merit a good wallop."

Vera sat on the edge of my bed.

I continued scrutinizing my bruises.

"I apologize for that. I've been in a rather *foul* mood for these past few days. It does seem that our grand opportunity may have slipped from our fingers... "

"That *is* a shame," I replied mirthlessly.

"It's obvious that we have no grounds to keep you, but we also cannot allow you to roam free. This is a very delicate operation, Peter—one that you inadvertently, I hate to say, helped to screw up in the most monumental way."

"Right," I glanced over my shoulder. "The next time a major corporation comes hunting for my friends without my prior knowledge or understanding, I'll be sure to feel bad."

Vera smirked. "Indomitable spirit."

"I don't know about all that." I looked in the mirror again, frowning. "But something about getting my arse kicked is toughening me up, I suppose."

"Speaking of that, I have an offer to make you."

I paused. My eyes flitted to hers in our reflection.

"What do you mean?"

Vera smiled. "Have you ever trained a dog?"

"Can't say that I have."

"Negative reinforcement never works with them. They simply refuse to respond to it, unless you consider *worse behaviour* a response. A dog cannot comprehend the meaning behind threats of physical violence—all that the dog knows is that it loves you, and you are angry. It cannot correlate its own actions to your responses. If it does something wrong, and you punish it, the dog has long since forgotten what it ever did in the first place, and acts submissively guilty simply to calm your anger."

"Am I the dog?"

"That's for you to decide," she smiled winningly. "So far, I have only been using *negative reinforcement* to get a result. It has not been working. In a *'Eureka!'* moment, I realized that what you might is a bit of pure incentive."

"Incentive?"

"You have two choices at the moment, Peter. In the first one, you remain in this cell. You will live in this cell, and one day, you will *die* in this cell, forgotten and *unseen.*"

"I'm not keen on that one…"

"In that instance, I'd like to ask you to come aboard."

"Sorry, what was that?"

"I realize now that I'm wasting an opportunity," the older woman conceded. "Logically, you would be of better use to me as a part of my team. You have actually *dealt* with a vampire, which is more than I could say for the rest of humanity. I could use a man who can meet with monsters and keep a *cheerful* disposition."

"So, you're saying you want me to… what? *Work* for you— as a part of Clover Pharmaceutical?"

"That is an oversimplification," she stated.

Unconvinced, I didn't shift my expression an inch.

"You want to see your friend again," Vera replied sweetly. "What better way is there to accomplish that than to be at my side? You'll never see her from the inside of this cell—but think on what we can achieve if we align our goals."

"Your goal is to suck a vampire dry."

"I only need enough blood to synthesize a similar compound. A pint would suffice. I assure you the vampire would come to no permanent harm… but is your worry truly for the safety of the vampire?"

My gaze turned away.

"Think about it," she continued, rising up from the bed. "What do you know of these creatures? What dark and magical influence did he have on your friend's sweet little mind? Do you trust your own feelings, now that he has taken her from you? Why were you so quick to accept the presence of a *monster*? Is it not *strange* that you showed no fear?"

"I… don't know what to say…" I replied, letting her words sink in.

"I'm giving you the opportunity to answer those questions. You will see the workings of my organization. It's a once-in-a-lifetime chance, Peter—and it is only being offered because of your *unique* experiences with a magical creature. That sort of experience is invaluable, but the information you hold cannot be allowed to exist outside of Clover…"

"Slow death… or a day job… this is a hard decision Vera."

"I want you as a personal aide, Peter," she replied, smiling fondly.

"Will I be on the payroll?"

"Of course," she smiled.

I paused. "I was *pretty sure* you'd say no…"

"Clover can offer you *anything* you desire. You'll receive a generous salary and your own condominium nearby," Vera informed, just as casually as someone suggesting Chinese takeout for dinner. "We *always* take care of our own… so long as I can trust you."

"What if I tried to run?" I asked, wincing at my own words.

"You won't run… because I think you want to understand what happened to your friend *just* as much as I do. I'll be back tomorrow. Don't disappoint me, Peter."

She rose from the bed and let herself out of my cell, leaving me alone with my thoughts—and not much else.

CHAPTER 29
CLARA

When I came to, I nearly threw up again.

But this time I was able to fight the sensation.

I swallowed the feeling and glanced around, trying to get my bearings. Flat, miserable tundra surrounded me as I stood on the side of a craggy slope, gazing upon a distant shelf of massive, jagged volcanoes. I thought at first that it was snowing, but it quickly occurred to me: *it's not snow... this is **ash***.

This was easily the most inhospitable place I'd ever seen—even the stars above were gone, blotted out with the sun by a thick layer of dark, smoggy clouds.

"This is The Wastes, isn't it?"

There was no answer.

With my sluggish brain I tried to recall which part of the world this was, back on my Earth.

Russia. All that is south of here is Alevorra, but the top half of the Asian continent is The Wastes...

That meant I was dealing with the elderly lord…

"Lord Vasiliev?" I called out. "Are you there?"

Once again, there was no immediate reply.

Shivering, I clenched my arms around myself. *She didn't just **leave** me out here… right? What sort of vampire lord would abandon me to the wilderness?*

I remembered my fleeting interactions with the oldest female vampire on the council, and I realized that I had my answer at hand. Every impression I'd gotten of Lord Valentine Vasiliev painted a gloomy picture—she *absolutely* struck me as the type to pull something like this.

I wonder how long I've been out here, wandering…

"I don't have much time!" I called out to the silence again.

It happened faster than I would have thought.

The world began to fade away…

৩১৩

IT FELT DIFFERENT THIS TIME.

For one, it didn't feel to me as if *any* time had passed—more so than usual, it seemed like I'd vanished in the blink of an eye. My surroundings had changed, so I took a few staggering steps.

I nearly tripped over a root, and I quickly planted my palm against a nearby tree to steady myself.

"Wait a minute…"

I cleared my eyes and gazed at the forest from my waking nightmares. "No. No, not now," I pleaded with whatever was listening. "How did this happen…?"

A voice came from nearby. "Hello, Clara."

I whirled around, hoping to see my grandmother.

The face that confronted me belonged to the lord of The Wastes, Valentine Vasiliev. Striding powerfully out from the trees, the vampire lord eyed me with malice.

"How are you *here*?" I asked in a panic.

The lord sneered. "The others may certainly satisfy themselves with merely interrogating you, but I had to see for myself."

"See what for yourself?"

"The forest. It is an *interesting* dream."

"How do you know about this place?"

She stopped to run her hand along a thick fern. "You have spoken of it at length with every lord. This nightmare is a consistent draw for you, it would appear—and it is buried so deeply within your mind that it took me a great amount of magic to coax it to the surface."

"This is a terrible and dangerous place," I shook my head. "We can't be here. I spend all my time trying to avoid it."

"Why is that? It doesn't seem so bad to me..."

"There's something in here with us," I pleaded with her. "I'm begging you, please just get us out of here."

"Something in here?" She narrowed her eyes.

I realized my mistake, but it was too late.

"We were about to make *such* progress, Clara... don't rob me of this now," the lord smiled evilly. "It seems you have forgotten the point of this trial—to dig into the deepest and darkest parts of you, when your personality has been suppressed. And *this*," she paused, motioning to the surrounding forest. "*This* is as deep and as *dark* as you can be..."

"I don't understand this place," I conceded in blind fear. "It has haunted my dreams for longer than I could remember. For a long time, something inside this forest would destroy me every time I closed my eyes. It chases me to the edge of a cliff, in view of an island, and then I'm torn apart, only to wake in my own bed."

"*What* chases you?" The lord asked darkly.

"I don't get to see it. It's a force of nature."

"Bring it to me."

"I don't want it to come."

Valentine Vasiliev began coming towards me. "You will *show me* the entity that stalks your deepest dreams—or you will pay the price for your lack of cooperation…"

"Please don't," I took a staggering step back. "I can't protect you…"

Her face contorted with fury. "Show me, Clara!"

"NO!" I screamed, losing control of my fury.

The forest ruptured around us; wood splintered out from trees and boughs as vines ripped apart. As the lord slipped backwards in the dirt, she began to crawl away from me. The world around us continued to rip apart as branches fell, roots upended, with splinters of their former glory filling the air…

I took a deep breath, trying to contain it—but it was no longer under my control, nor had it *ever* really been. It whipped around like an invisible predator, threatening to destroy us under its fury as it bore down *hard*…

"Clara, that's enough!" Lord Vasiliev demanded.

"I can't make it stop!" I called out to her.

"I've seen plenty, call it off!"

"It's coming for me!"

"Clara—"

The force descended—just as I felt it surge towards me, eager to rip me to shreds, I realized that Lord Vasiliev had crossed our gap. She held me back with an arm as she lifted up her free palm, roaring at the top of her lungs.

The force slammed into her magical defense. I sensed it snarl in confusion as it tried to whip around and crush me from a new direction, but the vampire lord shoved me aside.

"Get down!" She snarled.

I did as she ordered, and I flung myself against the floor of the dream forest. Covering my head, I looked up to see the vampire lord of The Wastes standing over me defensively; my unlikely ally wielding raw unbridled magic against the predator of my dreams.

"You need to let yourself go back under!"

"Back under what?"

"The spell! It's the only way to release us!"

"What? Why did you pull me in here if you couldn't get us out—?"

"Don't question it! Don't fight it! Just let the spell do its job and *drag us back out of here!*"

I tried to do as she ordered, but the sounds of the furious monstrosity were too much of a distraction. The predatory force would clearly stop at *nothing* to destroy me, and it was too overwhelming to relax my mind.

Wait, I thought.

I climbed up to my feet behind her.

"What are you doing?!" Lord Vasiliev snarled at me. "Get back down before you—"

"Take my hand!"

She was holding both palms up, barely restraining the abomination from attacking us. "What? *Why?*"

"Just do it! I know what has to be done!"

The lord shielded us both as the force rained down splinters and broken branches. With a reluctant grunt, she pulled one palm free and shoved it into my hand.

"Now *run!*"

I yanked at her arm, and she bolted after me.

"Why can't I run at proper speed?" She demanded.

"No idea! Elliott couldn't do it either!"

"Wait—how did he—?"

"Less talking, more running!"

We raced through the treeline and bolted towards the clearing I knew all too well—including the fact that it held nothing but a cliff that hung out over the ocean below...

I stopped her just short of the fall.

In the distance, the island awaited.

The vampire lord shuddered. "There is something *wrong* with that island..."

I didn't get a lot of time to consider that, as our time had run out. The force was just about to crush us...

"Is that Lord Craven?"

The dark silhouette of Elliott Craven stepped out of the trees, but I remembered the *last time* I'd seen that version of my savior in my dreams. He would not save me.

"Jump!" I snapped, grabbing her hand.

"What?" She turned my way.

"That's not Elliott—and you do *not* want see him up close and personal. Trust me, we have to *jump,* and we have to do it *now!*"

As if on cue, the nightmare burst from the trees, roaring

past the vision of Elliot and coming for us with an unimaginable fury. The nightmare forest roared around us and we leapt from the cliff—down towards the crushing waves of the ocean below.

Even with the adrenaline pumping in my veins, I could feel the suppressing effects of the spell coming for me…

CHAPTER 30
ELLIOTT

I stood with my arms folded in front of the portal.

The welcoming party was fanned out at the rear. To my sides stood my vassals, Nikki and Kinsey. Behind us, Clara's Knightly Trio awaited. I'd even dug up the high chancellor Silas and the sage of Stonehold, Sebastian, for the occasion.

All that was missing was Lorelei Craven.

The chrysm portal surged to life in a powerful flare; the gatekeeper turned her head towards me. "Incoming arrivals, Lord Craven."

"Perfect." I tensed my arms.

Within seconds, the portal flickered.

Out of the glowing tear in space stumbled…

"Clara!" Her friends blurted out.

She stepped forward, glancing around in a daze—as if she were seeing without sight or awareness. *That's **exactly** what's happening, isn't it Clara? What have they done to you?*

I took a few strides forward and pulled her into my embrace. She slumped against me wordlessly.

My eyes landed with incredible malice on the portal. Out from the chrysm surface came Lord Valentine Vasiliev, the dreaded matronly ruler of The Wastes. She glanced at us with an expression of blank horror. For all the good it would've done, I wanted to banish her from my island in that very instant.

Wilhelm and her trio came to our side. It wasn't a surprise that the three *immediately* knew something was deeply amiss. "Clara?" He asked tentatively. "Is… everything alright?"

"She cannot hear you," the dark lord of The Wastes coldly replied. As her eyes settled on my gaze, I realized that she was waiting for me to betray any knowledge of what they had done to her.

The lord looked rattled, and I didn't know why.

"Something is wrong," I told Lord Vasiliev. "Why is she sluggish and vacant like this?"

"Everything is as it should be, Lord Craven, and all shall be explained soon," the elderly vampire lord noted, turning her attention toward the portal. "The others will be here shortly. I must speak with them…"

"You three," I ordered the trio. "Help Clara."

They gladly intervened, pulling the spellbound girl away from the action. I watched as they sat her down on the stairs behind us; the wafting smoke from the portal along the floor parted as she plunked herself down, and it quickly enveloped her legs once again.

I turned back to Lord Vasiliev. "You assure me that she is fine? She looks stunned."

The vampire lord hesitated.

It was enough to make me question her.

"There is no reason to fear, Lord Craven."

"If any of you have injured Clara, *I* am not the one who should be in *fear*," I replied, my body filled with an angry rage unlike anything I'd experienced before. It was all I could do to contain myself. Antagonizing lord Vasiliev did me no service, but feigning ignorance was easy with this much anger within me. I suspected retribution would be swift if any of them, especially *her*, discovered that Lord Mattias had enlightened me of Clara's alarming condition.

Lord Vasiliev did not respond to my threat. The other lords began to arrive, allowing a merciful break from the deadly silence that had set in on the chamber. Within moments, the whole Council of the Eight Holds was standing in my portal chamber—minus Lord Akachi Azuzi, of course.

"Welcome back to Stonehold," I greeted them with as calm a voice as I could muster. "Before I ask about the results of the trial, who among you would like to explain to me why Clara Blackwell is wandering around like a mindless buffoon?"

☙❦❧

THE ENTIRE GROUP OF US—LORDS BLACKBURN, LOVRIĆ, KRUM, Vasiliev, Fire, Song, my sage, my high chancellor, Clara's trio of guards, my two vassals, Clara, and myself—made our way to the pavilion where so much had transpired.

This was where the sorceress and I cast a spell upon Clara that protected her from vampirekind—and spiraled her into a deep and magical coma.

It was also where we banished her from our world.

It was where we prepared our final stand when the vampire lords arrived on the island.

Now, we had come full circle....

The welcoming party hung back along the edges as Nikki and I confronted the lords. They dispersed in a circle around Clara, facing our dazed human guest.

"Join us, both of you," Ooktuk Krum ordered.

We did as he suggested, standing together in a gap left to fill out the circle. As he gave us specific orders of visualization and words to repeat, the assembled lords combined forces to pull Clara back out of her spellbound state. Even my own meagre magical talents seemed to be needed for this dangerous procedure...

The human began to glow as the light around us darkened in response. Soon, the slightest hint of a seal was present around her—and under our might, that seal cracked and vanished.

Clara took a stumbling step and began to fall.

I had her in my arms in an instant.

"Elliott?" She whispered in confusion.

"It's alright," I smiled. "I'm here..."

CHAPTER 31
GARRETT

S taring out the window of my cheap West Midlands flat, my eyes listlessly gazed out over the characteristic rain in the dark. Turns out, the rumours were true: England was the soggiest place I'd ever dared to step foot, and that went *double* for the land just outside Birmingham. The damned angels dumped their bathwater from on high, soaking us mere mortals in the flood.

*Well, they only have the **white** robes,* I recalled with a self-indulgent smile. *I suppose getting out the stains must be a nightmare...*

I never understood why others grew melancholic during the rain. It merely made me feel introspective; it helped me think. And *thinking* was precisely what I was doing now. With a tumbler of iced diet soda in my hand, I stared out into the rain and considered all that I had learned.

Vera knew that I could hear her. She knew that I'd stayed to watch her interrogation from the security room. I'd listened with rapt attention as she described the history of Clover and the Blackheart Circle.

But she hadn't said a word to me about it in the time since.

The revelations still had me reeling. For years, I'd tried to determine what my superior truly desired in her grand schemes—now I had my answer. We were seeking the blood of a magical creature... and we would use that blood to create something of staggering value.

A panacea for life itself... a chance at *immortality*.

That kind of power would give Clover incalculable power across the world.

That's what Vera Partridge wanted. She was looking for the same thing Clover had been chasing for untold years.

Power over life and death itself.

I'd given her ambitions the benefit of the doubt—but it didn't surprise me that, for all of my superior's discipline and drive, her goals came down to satisfying our most basic of human instincts: *survival*.

I was almost disappointed.

To think—after all of this, such a wonderfully brutish aim...

The revelations had shifted something near the bottom of my loyalty. A foundational stone budged, just a few inches wrong. It was enough to begin something. It made me wonder. It made me question.

But it made sense, and I had to give it to her. The plan fit entirely with what I knew of my enigmatic and tight-lipped master. I wondered what the rest of the board of directors would think, after she succeeded and rose above them. I could not fathom a world in which she failed.

But the question was... *when?*

The stolen boy had interfered. If he hadn't assisted our

wayward traveler and her vampiric friend, it would have been a creature from another world in our holding cell, not some smarmy British brat.

The rift was active, but only just barely. The second cycle was over. Something from this side had come and gone; something from *that* side had done the same. The traveler from our world left no trace; she (and the boy had told us it was, in fact, a *she*) had disappeared like the faintest whisper in a rolling storm, or perhaps a specter in the wafting of midnight smoke.

She was gone, as was the vampire. There was truly no telling when either would return to this world.

We only had *him* now...

I prided myself on being reasonable, and I was quite willing to offer credit where credit was due. At least the damned kid was smart—or smart *enough*. Just uttering the wrong thing to the esteemed Vera Partridge could have snuffed his life out in the blink of an eye, no matter his usefulness or lack thereof—but he'd made her laugh the night that their paths collided. He continued to entertain her twisted sensitivities, even though it took a little *encouragement* to get him in the mood to be... *talkative*. I could tell she was endeared to him, if only in the way you can enjoy a brand new toy.

In the way that a snake is endeared unto a live mouse...

Holding him against his will was *remarkably* illegal, but the mere act of capturing and containing him had been easier than I expected—especially for a country that prided itself on the endless scores of surveillance cameras. It was nearly embarrassing, really. The inefficiency of our operations had been hindered in absolutely no way by their grand and all-seeing eye…

The boy was smart. I knew he was. I could see it, plain as day, and I did so *every* day. I'd taken to relieving the attendant for lunch and having my meals seated in front of the security feeds. I liked to watch the prisoner over the feed; it was not a blind fascination, as I had little tolerance for inane 'guests'. Peter Tatham was starkly different. I could almost *see* his brain at work as he sat in the silent, lonely cell.

He looked like a textbook 'decent kid', like someone half-formed and ripped from the pages of a book. Peter struck me as the ideal young man, or at least the *shape* of one. The boy was nothing but a secondary character in his own story, a silhouette, molded incomplete—like clay that had not yet set beneath the scathing heat.

But the thing about clay is that it can be molded.

Something in his gaze told me that there was much more to this boy than first met the eye—and it made me truly begin to wonder if he could be pressed into a more suitable mold…

No, that was the wrong idea.

A better suggestion came to mind:

*What if he could be **honed?***

To torture or obliterate what he was and *force* him into a new point of view would be structurally unsound to the mind. To recast Peter Tatham would, as far as I could see, make him much less than the sum of his parts.

*But if we find a way to make him **pivot**… if we can slowly twist him into something new…*

For all his resilience and attitude, there was just the slightest wisp of darkness in that heart—a seed, ready to be planted. This seed did not take water and the sun. It needed shadows; and blood.

He did not see it, but I did.

And if *I* did, my superior must have picked up on it as well.

But what was it? What could be the thing upon which we make this boy one of our own? I had considered this conundrum half the night; the answer finally struck me with the changing of the guard in the sky. *Of course,* it finally dawned on me. *How could I be so foolish?*

The boy was *jealous.*

If he wasn't already, he could be *made* jealous.

He expressed some attachment for the girl we had come so close to meeting. It could not have been easy to turn away from proof of another world with the knowledge that you would never, ever see it for yourself...

And even if he had, even if he was so *selfless* that he had moved on for the greater good...

Yes, I smiled to myself. *I can undo that, can't I? I can take that away from you, Peter Tatham. I can bring you over to our way of thinking. What better way than to make it* **your** *choice?*

I almost felt bad at the prospect.

I wondered what would soon become of him when Vera Partridge, like a cunning cat playing with her prey, finally grew bored of his presence.

All of these thoughts came to a head when I finally recognized the breaking dawn through the dark. Setting the forgotten glass against the countertop, I gazed upon the sun and let out a weary sigh.

How was I up all night?

I glanced down at my smart-watch. The displayed time was early—or rather *late,* I suppose—and the date flickered in the corner, relieving me. "Oh, thank God," I chuckled mirthlessly. "Saturday. I nearly forgot..."

Freed from the shackles of a godforsaken day ahead of me, I tugged at the half-undone tie around my throat. I was trying them on for size, to see how they fit on me; I hadn't quite drawn a conclusion yet.

But what I *did* draw was a bath.

And as I undressed, neatly folding my clothes into a square on the edge of the bed, and as I silently settled down into the relaxing warmth of the steaming, claw-foot tub, I let go of all my numerous, nagging worries and uncertainties about this dark future ahead of me.

The woman can wait, I thought firmly. *The boy can wait. The goddamn worlds **themselves** can wait...*

I rested my head back to the porcelain and descended into the widening abyss of blissful nothingness. For a time, everything was as it should be.

CHAPTER 32
CLARA

The vampire lords stood gathered beneath the stars.

Mattias spoke: "Clara Blackwell, step forward."

Elliott held my hand, squeezing it tightly before he let me go. Turning to him, I let my gaze say everything I couldn't articulate in front of our judge and jury.

With my chin held high, I walked into their midst.

The lords watched from their semi-circle. I couldn't read the expressions on any of their faces; a foreboding feeling filled my heart as I swallowed awkwardly.

Lord Blackburn turned from lord to lord—clearly, he could read them far better than I. Finally, he turned back to me again. In his powerfully dark gaze, I realized that he might have never been on our side to begin with; Elliott had tried to warn me that these were cunning and highly manipulative creatures, after all.

"The judgment has concluded. Are you ready?"

"Yes, Lord Blackburn," I nodded quietly.

Everything around us seemed darker than usual. In the

company of these dreaded beings—who had shown me beautiful and interesting things, all while observing my actions beneath their spell—I felt the full intensity of their combined power.

Elliott was right to fear them, I thought sadly.

"We have met in private to freely discuss our separate findings," the lord told me. "At present, we decline the opportunity to share them—and we move to the proposals in one round of voting."

Nikki quickly opened her mouth to speak; Elliott, thinking swiftly, sharply jabbed an elbow into her ribs to stop her from upsetting the balance.

"Clara Blackwell... as a particularly magic-resistant entity you have entered our world *twice* on a whim, and gone so far as to pull a vampire lord from his own castle. You singularly represent a great deal of potential... and a great deal of chaos. We must now decide whether to treat you as a threat to the continued safety and security of this council. If there is a yea majority, you will be destroyed where you stand. Do you accept this judgement?"

Hesitantly, I tried to keep a brave face.

I nodded, and the votes came swiftly.

Ooktuk Krum: "Nay."

Svetlana Lovrić: "Nay."

Eyes-Like-Fire: "Nay."

Chanda Song: "Nay."

Mattias Blackburn: "Nay."

Valentine Vasiliev: "Nay."

A breath of relief escaped my lips. I didn't dare turn to look at Elliott's expression—nor did I avert my eyes to steal a look from any of my other friends here.

"You are hereby not to be considered a threat to this world, and will thusly not be considered as such," Lord Blackburn spoke with a small smile. "Now, we consider the next decision: Lord Craven tells us you are interested in advancing the innate magical power inside you. Is this true?"

"It is," I nodded respectfully. "I wish to study with a tutor from the Seven Portals."

"There are ways to learn magic in every hold," Lord Blackburn observed. "No matter where in the world that we place you, the opportunity will be forever present. As such, the proposal at hand is for you to be granted our blessing to pursue magical training. If there exists a yea majority, you will henceforth be granted the permission of the Council of the Eight Holds to study magic."

"I did not realize you could deny this," I replied in a crestfallen tone. *Could they really interfere with that?*

"Magic is a dangerous weapon in the right hands. You have already demonstrated the ability to resist *impossibly* powerful spells, even those cast by the strongest of the vampire lords. To allow you free reign could grant us all a dangerous enemy in the future—or a *powerful* friend."

Lord Blackburn turned to the others. "Choose."

Ooktuk Krum: "Nay."

Svetlana Lovrić: "Nay."

Eyes-Like-Fire: "Yea."

Chanda Song: "Yea."

Mattias Blackburn: "Yea."

Valentine Vasiliev: "Nay."

"It's a tie," Mattias observed. "In this case, we would default to the whim of Lord Akachi Azuzi, but our friend from the

Falvian Badlands remains deposed within the dungeons below. Instead, I propose a solution..."

The others turned to him curiously, just as I did.

"Instead of merely sending you a tutor, it occurs to me that perhaps you should learn on the premises. With a proper magical education, you would be taught how to *responsibly* wield your magic—and being submersed in the environment would likely advance your powers at a much more controllable rate. My proposal is for you to leave Stonehold Castle to undergo special training at the source."

I turned to Elliott with a terrified look. Wearily, his gaze met mine. *Will they wrench us away altogether?*

Lord Blackburn continued. "Choose."

Ooktuk Krum: "Yay."

Svetlana Lovrić: "Yay."

Eyes-Like-Fire: "Nay."

Chanda Song: "Yea."

Mattias Blackburn: "Yea."

Valentine Vasiliev: "Nay."

"It is decided," Lord Blackburn replied. "The human will not be permitted to stay within this castle, nor any of the others, while undergoing magical training."

My heart collapsed in my chest. *Surely we can find a way to beat that—there **has** to be a loophole somewhere...*

"Finally, we must decide upon the most important matter at hand. We've established that Clara Blackwell is not, for the time being, a danger to this world. In that vein, we chose to allow her to pursue magic, but only if committed to a place of proper training. You first appeared here, on the Isle of Obsidian, in the castle of the Craven family. Suffice for us to admit, a great deal of Lord Elliott's choices since that point have clearly revolved around maintaining your safety—and at times, to the detriment of cooperation..."

Elliott's confidence faltered, just barely.

"We overlook this, for the sake of making impartial decisions for the betterment of our realm. However," he continued, "this council agrees that Elliott Craven should not receive automatic control over your fate. He has resisted all of our attempts to meet you, and has often antagonized other lords in his single-minded commitment to keeping you inside *this* castle. A yea majority over this proposal will allow you to remain here, in Stonehold. Otherwise, we'll devise your new home among the other holds."

The moment of truth had finally come...

Silence descended upon all of us gathered. As the grave Lord Blackburn eyed me carefully, it felt like the weight of the entire world was poised to fall upon me.

"The time has come to we decide where you will stay, until such time as you choose to pursue your magical training," the lord continued with a cool gaze. "At hand, we have our final proposal: should we allow Clara Blackwell to remain here in Stonehold?"

Lord Blackburn opened up the vote. "Choose."

Ooktuk Krum: "Yea."

Svetlana Lovrić: "Yea."

Eyes-Like-Fire: "Nay."

Chanda Song: "Yea."

Mattias Blackburn: "Yea."

Valentine Vasiliev: "Nay."

My heart never beat harder than that moment. The vote from Lord Valentine didn't surprise me, but I felt a pang of betrayal from the tribal lord who now watched me with a prying, heartless gaze.

"It has been chosen," announced the vampire lord of Bleakwood. "Clara Blackwell—our human guest from beyond the edge of this world—this council has decided that you will stay in the care of Lord Elliott Craven, your first and *original* guardian, until such time as you choose to pursue your magical talents further. He must now swear to keep you protected at *all* times, as your life is arguable one of the most valuable on the face of this world."

"You are sending her to the Seven Portals for magical training," he replied sternly. "How might you propose that I keep her safe if I must remain in Stonehold?"

"Who says you have to stay on the island?"

Elliott paused. "It is tradition."

Lord Blackburn cast a gaze towards the nomad. "All of us turned a blind eye to the absentee nature of the lord from the Timberland Plains. If we can do that, then it is my firm opinion that you should be permitted to leave this castle at your desire. Remember, however, that your people are still in a vulnerable place concerning a recent trip to the human world you took. It might not be within your best interest to scamper off so quickly."

"That is a strong point," Elliott replied. "Might I ask for a concession, then?"

"Name it, and we will decide."

He turned to the rest of the gathered group—and in particular, to my Knightly Trio. Nikki stood among my friends as well, where she belonged.

"My request is two-fold," Elliott noted.

"Then hope we are generous," Valentine scoffed.

Elliott ignored that. "Clara holds kinship with three guardians that I appointed to her—all of them former royal guards within this castle. I ask permission to send them back into duty with her, and to allow them to join her at the Seven Portals."

Lord Blackburn raised an eyebrow. "I can't think of any reason to deny that. What say you, my lords?"

They all agreed.

*I'm so happy that I could **kiss** you again...*

"My second request may not be so easy to grant. These guards, while themselves greatly affectionate towards their charge, have proven incapable of protecting her against all potential dangers," Elliott spoke carefully. "It occurs to me that a fourth guardian might not be out of the question if I am asked to ensure her personal safety."

"Who do you choose?" Lord Blackburn enquired.

Elliott turned to his sister.

Wait—Elliott, what are you—?

"Nikki Craven is *powerful* in the use of wild magic, and she is a capable protector of the mainland. She has spent a *century* in single combat with the most vicious beasts and traitorous vampires that Stonehold has to offer—all without *official* magical training. The magisters denied her approval to Seven Portals, and she was forced to hone her talents in the Far Reaches..."

His gaze shifted back to the vampire lords.

"I ask for permission to send my sister with Clara and her guardians as well—to finally allow her to receive a sanctioned education, and to help the others *protect* her."

The lords went silent as they looked between us all.

"This is an unusual request," he finally replied.

"It is a compromise in line with your wishes. I can think of no better way to keep Clara safe."

"Lords, you have heard him. What do you say?"

Ooktuk Krum: "Nay."

Svetlana Lovrić: "Nay."

Eyes-Like-Fire: "Yea."

Chanda Song: "Yea."

Mattias Blackburn: "Yea."

Valentine Vasiliev: "Nay."

Lord Blackburn sighed. "We have a tie once again. However, I do not have a rectification in mind this time. What about the rest of you?"

They all shook their heads.

"Then the compromise shall be this, Lord Craven—we will not forbid it, but we do not condone it. If you choose to follow this path, we will not exercise our right to enforce it with the academy. The ultimate decision shall remain theirs."

"I'm willing to take that compromise," Elliott replied warmly.

"Do you have any other requests? Think wisely."

Elliott Craven confidently folded his arms over his chest, as usual. "I do not wish to *test* the generosity that has been shown to us tonight. Consider this matter concluded."

"What of the rest of you?" Lord Blackburn turned to the other vampire lords. "Speak now, or never."

Each of them gazed toward me, but none spoke. Whatever secrets they had learned in their time with Clara, it was clear that they intended to keep them locked away...

"Very well then," the lord of Bleakwood nodded. "In that note, I hereby conclude this meeting of the Council of the

Eight Holds. The matter of Clara Blackwell's fate is henceforth and forever over..."

Elliot spoke up. "I greatly appreciate your fairness in these decisions. You have my word that I will uphold the decree of the Council of the Eight Holds. In closing this meeting, I request that the assembled lords stay here in Stonehold for one final night. We have yet to address the passing of my mother, and I invite you all to attend her final service."

CHAPTER 33
NIKKI

The entire castle was assembled in the gardens as Elliott took his position on the pavilion. I stood to the side with the assembled vampire lords, watching supportively. Nearby, still looking worse for wear, Clara waited quietly.

There are so many delightful victims here...

I swallowed. *I don't have time for this right now. Please.*

Oh, it snarled in my head, *you haven't been listening to me at **all** these past few days. Why won't you let me help you? We're supposed to be a team—and you're not holding up your end, are you...?*

I steeled myself. *We will talk soon—not now.*

***Why** not now?*

Because right now, I replied, *I need to see my mother.*

The whisper retreated, and I sighed in relief.

I felt a hand on my shoulder. When I turned, it was Clara. She smiled sadly, as if *really* seeing me—and even sensing the conflict that bubbled in my head. I offered her a brave smile in return. She nodded quietly, released her grip, and looked away.

I felt reassured... somehow.

"Thank you all for joining us," my brother's voice boomed out across the crowd. "We have gathered here today, all of us —those of us natively on this island, esteemed guests from the Stonehold mainland, and the vampire lords from the farthest corners of our world—to memorialize one of the greatest vampires in our long history... my mother, Lorelei Craven."

Elliott paused then, looking out over the crowd.

It must have been daunting to see them all here. The better half of a thousand vampires stood gathered to pay their respects to the deceased.

"Lorelei was a proud woman," he offered the crowd. "She was a dedicated ruler, a complicated mother, and a resolute guardian above all. She lays dead today because she gave her life in service of not only this hold, but also our entire world. We owe her a powerful debt of gratitude, one that can never be repaid."

He sighed heavily, staring at the covering shroud in front. Beneath that white cloth laid our mother's corpse, placed on a stone block as per the traditions.

"Mother was never one to mince words, or to revel in her own accomplishments, but it goes without saying that her time and endeavors have benefitted all of us in greater ways than I can possibly explain. She was the greatest peacekeeper to step foot on the world stage. She dedicated her life to bettering our own—in everything from the development of chrysm as a source of power and a means of travel, to forging the current era of enlightenment that Stonehold has enjoyed for *centuries*. It goes without saying that life on this world would be much darker for the rest of us, had Lorelei Craven never taken root."

A low rise of sound began from the crowd, but Elliot silenced it.

"But she was not one for empty praise; and she didn't suffer fools. Lorelei Craven prepared her successors to follow that same path, even as she worked to negotiate alliances and defend our people from dangers beyond our comprehension. In her memory, I will concede the stage to one who helped Lorelei in carefully maintaining the balance of our world. Lord Blackburn, if you would…"

Mattias broke rank and strode up to the stage with a brave face. He'd never explained to us why he seemed to take our mother's death to heart—I held my suspicions, but it wasn't wise to state them without proof.

Elliot gave him a fierce, respectful nod as they crossed paths; then, he joined me at my side.

Each lord in turn took the stage to deliver their own eulogies for the fallen Craven. There was nothing I could say that Elliott hadn't, and the last thing I needed was to lose my fleeting self-control in front of all these vulnerable vampires.

After the last lord spoke, Elliott moved to retake the stage again—but Clara stopped him.

"Can I say something?" She asked him.

He looked surprised. "Are you sure?"

"I think it's only right that I do."

Elliott shared a look with me; and he nodded.

With our blessing, Clara Blackwell strode up to the pavilion and took her place behind the mourning slab. She turned to face the sea of vampires; I smiled as I saw the fear and regret cloud her tentative expression.

Yet, the human toughed it out.

"Many of you have merely *heard* of my existence," she addressed the silent, collected throng. "My name is Clara Blackwell. I am a human who joins you here from beyond this world. I wanted to give my own parting words to Lorelei Craven—a woman who never took advantage of me, and who always treated me with respect..."

This ought to be good, I thought curiously.

She let her gaze drop to the veiled body before her.

"Lorelei... I met you the very day that I first arrived in this world. When I found myself here, I was terrified and alone. I didn't know where I was, why I was here, or why everything —from your skies to your gardens—looked more beautiful than anything I'd ever experienced. You didn't know what to make of me, and in that confusion you were distant and callous at times... but we spent time together, you and I, and there was one thing that always stuck out to me."

Clara glanced up to Elliott and me.

"You loved your *children*. You loved your *subjects*. You loved *me*. In some strange way, I believe you loved every vampire that roams this world, no matter their allegiance. You loved them with all of your heart. You were quite willing to do *anything*, no matter the cost, to keep us all protected. It's fitting that we find ourselves here, surrounded by the beautiful gardens you planted with your own two hands. This incredible place is a telling testament to the strength of your heart. The very flowers resist the endless winter, showing us their beautiful color against the snow. Lorelei, you have made a beautiful mark upon this world, and it speaks of your loss, your compassion, and your conviction."

The lords watched carefully as Clara continued.

"If you were here, Lorelei, you'd be angry that I was speaking of this... but I think it's only right that I tell the world of your love. We've all heard of your strength and your commitment to maintaining order, but I think the most important thing about you, to me, is the love that was in your heart. You had so much to give to all of us, in your own *special* way—and I want all those who intend to witness your final rest to understand that. You gave your life so that peace may flourish. May your flowers always bloom."

She glanced up from the shroud. "Thank you."

A quiet clap came from nearby. I turned to see the lord of The Drenchlands, Lorelei's close friend Svetlana Lovrić, was showing her approval.

Mattias began clapping as well.

Then came someone in the crowd, and another...

Within moments, the entire procession applauded Clara Blackwell's eulogy. The human looked surprised as she stood up on the platform, presented with hundreds upon hundreds of vampires who respected her words...

Elliott and I led the vampire lords to the slab. Together, we moved the remains of Lorelei Craven to the open stone coffin that was held suspended in the air by our magic.

With Clara at our back, we brought my mother into the center of the memorial gardens. There, at the sprawling roots of the most imminent tree, the lords and I parted the earth and set the lidless coffin down to join the one that was already there, sealing in a magical wave of soil and roots.

"This garden was where our mother passed from this world," Elliott remarked to us in private, "and it was her favourite place on the planet to be. She loved Fiona with all her heart and built this place to memorialize her forever. It makes perfect sense, then, to bring them together in death—and to plant her bones here, in her most beloved place, so that her memory may live on."

I nodded. "It's exactly what she would've wanted."

Mattias spoke: "And so, your duty ends."

"And so, your duty ends," Svetlana repeated.

"And so, your duty ends," Valentine nodded.

"And so, your duty ends."

"And so, your duty ends."

"And so, your duty ends."

Each of the vampire lords paid their final respects, one at a time, until Elliott took my hand in his; we sank to our knees at the grave of our mother, briefly turned to one another, and then repeated together:

"And so, your duty ends…"

CHAPTER 34
ELLIOTT

The vampire lords were finally ready to return to their holds. Nikki, Clara, and I saw them off at the portal.

Each one offered their goodbyes, and a few congratulated Clara on her bright, new future. The two lords who stuck behind, were Mattias and Svetlana. Once all of the others had passed through the portal, the two of them spoke to us privately.

"We are taking Lord Akachi with us," Mattias noted. "He is no longer your responsibility to hold within these castle walls. Has he been fed in our absence?"

"No," I answered bluntly.

"Good," Svetlana replied thoughtfully. "Now that it has been a week since he's had blood, the lord should be far too weak to retaliate when we awaken him."

"Tell me you aren't doing that here."

Mattias shook his head. "Of course not. He's proven

himself an irrevocable danger to Stonehold. Personally, we don't want him anywhere *near* this castle until we've properly judged and penalized him for his crimes."

"Will I need to be a part of that?"

"You can decline," Svetlana shrugged. "However, it should be an entertaining trial. You might even find the experience to be cathartic, given your history…"

I hugged Clara close to me. "I think I'll pass. I've had enough of *trials* for the time being."

Svetlana thinned her lips, but Mattias laughed.

My sister cut in with a curiously apprehensive look. "You know, something's been bothering me…"

"What would that be?" Svetlana asked.

"There have been hints of a unifying threat—one strong enough to rally you together behind our cause. We know that our mother was convinced that some kind of disaster is on its way, but I have to ask: what does the council think of this? Do we need to prepare?"

Svetlana Lovrić contemplated this for a moment.

"You mean the Calamity."

"The Calamity?" Clara asked, tilting her head.

"Lorelei Craven's knowledge came from looking past the Pierced Veil," Svetlana recalled, as if warning us. "She believed that the old stories were all tied together—the Cataclysm, the Sanguine Ones…"

"And she thought it would happen again?" I asked.

"Remember that we have no proof it ever happened in the first place. If there ever *were* any Sanguine Ones, all genuine proof of their existence has been lost to history. It is not scientifically sound to consider them a fact."

"Assume for a moment that it's all true," I spoke quietly. "If

Lorelei was right… if, once upon a time, there really *was* a Cataclysm that birthed our world…"

"Those are large *if's*," Svetlana noted dryly.

I continued anyway. "What would happen if there was a *second* Cataclysm—this Calamity?"

Svetlana pursed her lips reluctantly. "The last time I spoke to her, Lorelei taught me a rhyme."

"A rhyme? Do go on," my sister smirked.

"The theory, of course, is that the Cataclysm swept away life on this world and rebuilt it to serve us. So then it stands to reason, given the rhyme—"

"Wait," Clara cut in. "I've read about it before."

"About the Cataclysm? Do you have information of it on your world, Clara?" Svetlana's interest was piqued.

"There's a book I found," she replied. "It was a tome of ancient magical history. I came across it tucked away in a library on my world."

"I thought there *was* no magic on your world."

"There isn't, but according to this book, there *used* to be. Something happened to take it away—the Cataclysm. I think that the stories here got it wrong—the Cataclysm didn't destroy your world… It's how your world was created."

"You think our worlds were connected?"

"I think it's a strong possibility."

Svetlana suddenly looked troubled. "If that is true, the Calamity would spell untold devastation, if Lorelei's knowledge is true. It casts that rhyme in a very dark light."

"Let me hear this 'rhyme'," I crossed my arms.

The scientist lord paused, reflecting on the words, and then she stated:

First came the Cataclysm in its blight
    Broken apart, divided in our plight
    The beasts grew proud
    The black wind howled
    Until Calamity doth reunite

"Beasts grew proud?" Nikki paused. "In all my years fighting monsters, they have never been more dangerous than they are now. The magic within them has twisted and changed—they've been getting more vicious, and a *damned* sight harder to kill."

Clara and I shared a horrified look for a very *different* reason.

We'd heard this rhyme before...

"What's wrong?" The stoic façade of Mattias Blackburn began to steadily crack; he comprehended our expressions with a rising look of confused horror. "Do you two *recognize* that rhyme?"

"The shadow creature in my dreams..." Clara's face was stricken with terror as she turned back to me again. "Elliott, the dream thing that looks just like you... the last time I saw it... just before we found our way back here again..."

"Yes," I realized gravely. "It was speaking in riddles within your dream... but the nightmare ended before the rhyme could finish. There are nearly ten thousand vampires here—but Clara's world is filled with more than seven *billion* humans, and weapons beyond any vampire lord's ability to comprehend. If the Cataclysm broke our worlds apart and separated our civilizations..."

Clara swallowed down her fear as the implications slowly dawned upon us. "Then the Calamity could bring them back *together...*"

CHAPTER 35
SABINE

I t was quite the adjustment, being alive again.

There existed no vessel for my return greater in magnificence than the body of a vampire lord.

As soon as I overwhelmed the stubborn lord on the ethereal plane I laid claim to his flesh. It had taken little to break the binding seals around him... after all, they were tied to his essence—and Lord Akachi Azuzi slumbered in the back of his own head.

For now, there was only *me*.

The Cravens were fools to have bound him into the same cell where I had been held. *Then again, that was a part of the plan, wasn't it? Influence Elliott Craven, forcing him to make that vital mistake...*

Of course, it had not been me to do it.

Elliott was marked—just like his *witch*.

My master had other servants; I knew myself to be one cog in a greater machine. While I was oblivious to the full extent of his machinations, I was aware of a few things...

Clara Blackwell had been infected through her very dreams.

The human had spread the infection to her beloved vampire lord—and for now, Elliott could be very subtly influenced.

All we needed was to find a way to pull that deranged *sister* of his under our growing power. In life, Nikki Craven had become my mortal enemy. I was willing to let bygones be bygones if she could be fashioned into an appropriate *weapon* —both with the powerful magic at her disposal, and the mental duress that plagued her.

If she could be turned to us, we'll have her forever.

I laughed at the thought, considering how much I would enjoy using her body as a vessel for my own mind. Certainly it would be more *entertaining* than this old and decrepit flesh that I found myself inhabiting…

My magic thrummed at my fingertips, powered by the miserable old vampire lord's body and his powerful blood. *How foolish have I been,* I thought hungrily, *to think I had ever known true power before now? With my innate sorcery and the incredible flesh and blood of a vampire lord within my grasp, I will be unstoppable…*

I couldn't let my newfound addiction to this powerful feeling rob me of my priorities. I had to get Lord Azuzi out of Stonehold. It was clear that this body had been starved and weakened in its time here. As long as I was stuck here, I would only get weaker with each passing day. Clearly, there were stark *limitations* to my power.

I heard movement nearby, and I closed my eyes.

It was cathartic to possess the taken flesh of my former master. Lord Azuzi in his ancient hubris saw fit to banish me from the Falvian Badlands, and I'd spent a very, *very* long time infiltrating Stonehold to find a spot near the Craven family. I had grand and *terrible* plans, but nothing I could have imagined would have put me in this cell, ready to strike...

My eyes stayed closed as I felt a strong presence.

"Lord Azuzi... you have missed a great deal," a raw and powerfully stern voice spoke. "Once we bring you to the Council of the Eight Holds and reawaken you, you shall be brought back up to speed..."

A name danced at the edge of my mind.

Mattias.

I resisted the urge to smile. I didn't have to lift a *finger* to escape this prison. A vampire lord had come to *personally* take this body away from the Isle of Obsidian.

This was the reward for my patience. My new master had delivered my promised salvation. I would fulfill my end of the bargain. This body had been given to me to bring just one thing to this miserable plane of existence...

Calamity.

APPENDIX

A Witch Between Worlds involves a vampire world very similar to our own, but with different names for many of the places, and certain striking differences. Some of my darling readers have asked that I add some sort of glossary for easy reference.

The following pages offer various details that may help you distinguish the distant regions and rulers of Elliott's realm—along with *trivia not yet touched upon*.

I hope it all makes for a compelling read!

-Emma Glass

HOLDS

Elliott Craven's world does not have kings, and thus any kingdoms or republics. Instead, it is divided into eight **holds**, which serve the same basic purpose.

In earlier times, there were more holds than the eight—but civil war and conquest has obliterated some of these places from the history books, and their history is sadly lost to time.

Each hold features an ancient vampire civilization of great power, separated by vast distances and untamed wilderness for all of history. Thanks to the discovery of *chrysm*, the distances between the holds have been rendered irrelevant, and the past two centuries have brought much progress in uniting the world of Vampires.

❦

Stonehold, or *Europe,* is where our story has largely taken place so far. Characterized by its trades, all walks of labourers toil away on the mainland—from blacksmiths to woodworkers to miners. Until the past few centuries, it was a relatively poor but proud worker economy. To the distant southeastern corner lay the **Far Reaches,** known for untamed wilderness and mystical gypsy tribes.

The civilization is now experiencing the tail end of a renaissance period, thanks to the revolutionary discovery of a powerful ore called *chrysm*, located here in abundance; the **Dawning Mines** in the southern **Alpine Ridge** are of particular wealth, carefully hidden from the world.

The seat of power is **Stonehold Castle** on the distant **Isle of Obsidian**, filled with vicious forests and countryside; you may know it as the *United Kingdom.* The sudden abdication of the throne by the beloved vampire lord Lorelei Craven has caused a crisis around her young and inexperienced heir, Elliott.

◈❀◈

The Falvian Badlands, or *Africa,* is a wild land divided into three major regions. The northern third is a largely inhospitable desert; the center is a dangerous jungle; the bottom third is a foreboding swamp. Along the eastern edge runs a stark and dangerous mountain range, filled with volcanoes and chaotic lightning storms. Such a threatening environment has hardened the vampires into a vicious, self-serving people —the land is rife with thieves, bandits, outlaws, and all manner of renegades.

As the Middle East exists in another form in this world, the **Gold Coast**—what would be our world's *Cairo*—rests on the shoreline as the merchant capital of the world. Of the rampant voodoo far south, the major landmark is ***Slough's***

Descent, a mystical swamp settlement near a massive canyon of tumbling bog and glowing silt (it is known to us as our largest waterfall, *Victoria Falls*).

The main castle, the foreboding **Tower of Scorch** of the **Killing Peaks**, rests atop the most active volcano of both worlds, *Mount Nyamuragira*. The intense lava flow here is restrained by ancient magic, used as a power source.

※

The Drenchlands, or *the Middle East,* is an archipelago of resource-stripped islands above a shallow sea. Stories tell of a time that the land was fertile and rich—but that a broken accord with nature resulted in a powerful flood that trapped the vampires on these newly formed arid islands.

Eons of overpopulation and poverty resulted in a society that encouraged intelligence and shrewdness to solve their many problems. Vampiric geniuses—with lifespans far less limited by death—have dedicated their years to the advancement of science, culminating in discoveries that have allowed their society to settle beneath the waves.

Little is known of the vampires of the Drenchlands since disappearing below the surface—only that they hold the most powerful technologies in the world. Their castle is the **Sunken Citadel**, built near the place where our world's Babylon sat.

※

Timberland Plains, or *America/Mexico,* is a widespread tribal land filled with every geographical option under the sun.

Rolling hills, soaring mountain ranges, vast plains, parched deserts, and icy valleys fill this region.

Settlements are few and far between—the nomadic vampires of the Timberland Plains chase the hunt and move with the herds of powerful magical creatures. As a result of their respectful bond with nature, in no small part due to powerful rituals and tributes to the stars, the wildlife works in conjunction with these vampire tribes and does not lash out at them like in other holds.

Of the few permanent settlements is the castle in the desert, the **Twilight Gate**—an imposing clay fortress atop a massive sandstone bluff, built as a sacred tribute to nature. It was known in our world as *Acoma Pueblo* of present-day New Mexico, or the *Sky City*.

᳇

Bleakwood, or *Canada,* is a frigid northern landmass of hunters, trappers, and miners. The endless sea of forest complicates the profession—it is haunted to the point of open hostility with all manners of wraiths, ghouls, and banshees. Furthermore, the natural wildlife is among some of the most cunning in the realm.

Vampires here seek what little warmth they can find in cavernous settlements of the western mountain ranges, such as the subterranean **Cavern's Solace**. The greatest among these people are explorers, carving their legacies out in the frozen and threatening woods—but even they dare only to explore along the edges.

The hold is ruled from **Blackburn Manor**, owned across

the ages by the eponymous family. It sits on the edge of a permanently frozen lake, what we call *Lake Louise*.

෴

Selvara Karn, or *South America,* has been overwhelmed by their world's equivalent of the *Amazon Rainforest.* Within the tropical forests breed limitless predators and swarms, empowered by unopposed magic. This greatly mystical hold, in fact, is widespread considered to be the most openly antagonistic one in the entire world. Very few to step foot there are ever heard from again.

The surviving vampires hole up in large settlements; the shamans and witch doctors of Selvara Karn harness the powerful magic that makes their lives so dangerous. It is thought that the potency of magic here is unrivaled.

World's Pillar, a towering tree akin to *Yggdrasil* of Norse mythology in the heart of *Amazonia,* serves as the major settlement and the fortified home of the vampire lord. The tree itself rises far above the forests; the shamanic colony exists as a treetop paradise, built upon the lesser trees that spout above its greatly magical roots.

෴

Alevorra, or *Southern Asia,* is a tropical paradise. Unlike Selvara Karn's rainforest gone wildly amok, Alevorra is filled instead with docile grasslands, secluded valleys, and gentle rainforests. The region enjoys diverse magical wildlife and a certain level of peace not typically seen on this world—

however, a natural balance is retained with the presence of strong magical monsoons.

This region is dotted with weathered temple ruins from a time long forgotten, forming most of the settlements. One such is **Lights Fall**, half-destroyed and falling apart, called *Bagan* in what we consider *Myanmar* or *Burma*.

Another easy Selvara Karn comparison is that the castle itself is the largest settlement. Our world's *Angkor Wat* of the fallen *Khmer Empire* lives on deep in the jungles as **Sunstone Temple**. Despite nature's attempts to reclaim the tempe, the widespread city center enjoys prosperity, sustaining itself with nearby agriculture and farming.

᪥

The Wastes, or *Russia and surrounding territories,* enjoys secrecy to a degree rivaling even the Drenchlands. Little is known of the hold, with only its geography—a dark, frozen scar of tundra and mountains ripped across the world—being well recorded.

Menacing and chaotic, the Wastes are considered a glum and inhospitable wasteland that forces its citizens into safety below the world, a lifestyle further complicated by the many, *many* active volcanoes that blight the horizon. It is said that the ash in the clouds above The Wastes forever blots out the sun and the stars.

The only known place of refuge within the Wastes is the **Nether Pit,** a subterranean castle of unknown origin.

VAMPIRE LORDS

The **vampire lords** are the fearsome monarchs of their world, each ruling a separate hold. The bloodlines of the vampire lords are energized with a powerful magic that, for better or worse, strengthens their innate abilities far beyond common vampires.

Together, they form the **Council of the Eight Holds**. It is from a hidden neutral zone, bound by restrictive magic, that they make decisions that affect the entire world.

It is through a powerful ritual called the **Ascension** that a vampire lord unlocks his or her untapped potential. If a lord is toppled and the bloodline wiped out, the hold as it is known is annexed by its conqueror, and the world's magic steadily takes care of the rest.

⊗✿⊗

Elliott Craven of **Stonehold** is the newest and youngest vampire lord in the world. After his beloved predecessor

Lorelei Craven suddenly abdicates the throne, her son is thrust vastly unprepared onto the world stage.

Cold, calculating, and greatly concerned with protecting his people, it is increasingly clear that his love for Clara Blackwell has radically changed his path.

His castle is **Stonehold Castle** on the **Isle of Obsidian.**

❧

Akachi Azuzi of the **Falvian Badlands** is eldest among the vampire lords. Ruling over a hold known for nearly constant chaos, warfare, and greed, Akachi has survived countless mutinies against his life for the throne.

A weathered, gnarled ebony vampire with a trickster's smile knows that he grows ever older, and seeks greater power to secure his grip over his anarchic realm.

His castle is the **Scorched Tower** of the **Killing Peaks.**

❧

Svetlana Lovrić of **The Drenchlands** respects only two things in this world: curiosity and ingenuity. Famously as reclusive as her subaquatic hold, Svetlana's scientific conquests power the world's technological infancy.

An odd friendship with Lorelei Craven directly led to the similarly minded vampires sharing the forefront of the recent chrysmic revolution.

Her castle is **Sunken Citadel** hidden beneath the sea.

❧

Eyes-Like-Fire of the **Timberland Plains** is a warrior maiden first and a vampire lord second. The tribal lord, her face riddled with bone piercings and tattoos, is quite happy to abandon her own castle to lead majestic hunts.

Her region, in no small part due to a love for the hunt, experiences a disproportionate count of slain vampire lords. Second in youth and tenure only to Elliott Craven, Eyes-Like-Fire feels a reluctant, distant kinship to him.

Her castle is the **Twilight Gate** atop an unnamed mesa.

❦

Mattias Blackburn of **Bleakwood** is the most physically imposing of the vampire lords. As unspoken ruler of the Council of the Eight Holds, his impartiality has kept his more volatile colleagues in line for centuries.

After Lorelei's abdication, his reign is now the longest in the world. Unbeknownst to the rest due to ancient law, he is secretly the father of her children.

His castle is **Blackburn Manor** near a solidified ice lake.

❦

Ooktuk Krum of **Selvara Karn** is the most enigmatic of the vampire lords. Ooktum chooses to listen rather than to speak —with his motives unknown, an air of mystery has enveloped the shamanic lord.

Surrounded by the mystical arts, even temporary allies are nervous of this quiet lord who keeps under control—*somehow* —the most naturally hostile hold in the world.

His castle is **World's Pillar** beneath a gigantic tree.

⚜

Chanda Song of **Alevorra** is a fairly new addition to the vampire lords, with a reign under three centuries. Equal in melodic beauty and caustic wit, the sarcastic Chanda is quick to mock—but slow to support another lord.

The peace across her hold gives Chanda a complete lack of ambition that rivals even Eyes-Like-Fire—but their conflicting hobbies keeps the two from being friends.

Her castle is **Sunstone Temple** in an ancient city ruin.

⚜

Valentine Vasiliev of **The Wastes** is an openly brutal and aggressive vampire lord, bordering on malevolence. The second-eldest lord to Akachi Azuzi, these two would make a formidable alliance—if they could ever agree.

Cold and antagonistic as her own bitter hold, Valentine rules an emptier realm than most. With the inexplicable arrival of the human, perhaps she senses *opportunity…*

Her castle is the **Nether Pit** beneath the volcanic tundra.

28271399R00162

Printed in Great Britain
by Amazon